*For the life of her, she could not look away
from the sparkling liquid
sluicing over his naked back.*

He resembled Poseidon rising from the sea, but a thousand times more appealing in the flesh than on the printed page.

The wind came up all at once. Colt's skin pebbled with the chill as he stepped out of the pool. She squeezed her eyes shut and buried her face in her arms.

She'd had no idea that she had it in her to be so rude.

Drops of water pattered on her hiding place. She heard one smack a leaf over her head...she felt one hit her scalp.

"Like to join me?" Colt's voice crooned.

She opened her eyes to see ten toes wriggling in the dirt in front of the bush.

She looked up, inch by inch. A respectable woman would have fled from the scene when she first saw him, not continue to ogle him.

And now she'd been caught.

* * *

Rebel Outlaw
Harlequin® Historical #1191—July 2014

Author Note

I would like to tell you how much it means to me that, in your busy life, you have chosen to set aside a bit of time to escape into the world of Holly Jane and her protector, Colt Wesson.

In this book, we travel back in time to a place called Friendship Springs, but reader beware, friendship has fallen by the wayside in this town.

This tale deals with a pair of feuding families, lovers dodging the cross fire and the young people of both families who defy their elders in an attempt to bring peace to a town that has been long torn apart by hatred.

Thank you for coming with me for Holly Jane and Colt Wesson's pursuit of love and a peaceful place to live.

I hope their story leaves you smiling.

Best wishes and happy reading.

CAROL ARENS

—

REBEL OUTLAW

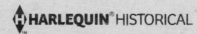
HARLEQUIN® HISTORICAL

Recycling programs
for this product may
not exist in your area.

ISBN-13: 978-0-373-29791-7

REBEL OUTLAW

Copyright © 2014 by Carol Arens

This edition published by arrangement with Harlequin Books S.A.

For questions and comments about the quality of this book, please contact us at CustomerService@Harlequin.com.

Printed in U.S.A.

CAROL ARENS

While in the third grade, Carol Arens had a teacher who noted that she ought to spend less time daydreaming and looking out the window and more time on her sums. Today, Carol spends as little time on sums as possible. Daydreaming about plots and characters is still far more interesting to her.

As a young girl, she read books by the dozen. She dreamed that one day she would write a book of her own. A few years later, Carol set her sights on a new dream. She wanted to be the mother of four children. She was blessed with a son, then three daughters. While raising them she never forgot her goal of becoming a writer. When her last child went to high school she purchased a big old clunky word processor and began to type out a story.

She joined Romance Writers of America, where she met generous authors who taught her the craft of writing a romance novel. With the knowledge she gained, she sold her first book and saw her lifelong dream come true.

Carol lives with her real-life hero husband, Rick, in Southern California, where she was born and raised. She feels blessed to be doing what she loves, with all her children and a growing number of perfect and delightful grandchildren living only a few miles from her front door.

When she is not writing, reading or playing with her grandchildren, Carol loves making trips to the local nursery. She delights in scanning the rows of flowers, envisaging which pretty plants will best brighten her garden.

She enjoys hearing from readers, and invites you to contact her at carolsarens@yahoo.com.

Chapter One

"You're an insult to the Travers name, Colt Wesson." Colt watched his cousin's hand flex then reach for the gun in his well-worn holster. "A low-down burr in the crotch of your pappy's pants."

He figured Cyrus wouldn't actually shoot him any more than Colt would draw his knife from the sheath slung across his back and slice his cousin's tongue in half.

Still, the threat deserved a response, so he reached over his shoulder and fingered the hilt of the long Arkansas Toothpick.

The last hot breath of summer settled upon the ranch. Dust covered everything from the rotting boards of the front porch to a saddle dangling over the corral fence. Even the flies spinning about manure piles seemed coated with it.

In the twelve years since he'd walked away from his boyhood home, nothing had changed. Colt glanced about the run-down buildings that made up the Broken Brand. Today, just as they had throughout his childhood, derelict-looking relatives lounged on the bunkhouse porch rolling and smoking cigarettes. They yawned, stretched and ignored the chores that would make the ranch a fit place to live.

"Pappy Travers ain't even moldering yet and you're lighting out again." Cyrus took a long step forward and glared up into Colt's face. "T'ain't right for you to cast aside family obligation."

He hadn't cast aside family obligation. If he had, he'd have brought the law with him to oust out this gang of thieves. Seeing his pappy properly buried was the only thing that had brought him home…that and the old ladies.

"You take the job of head outlaw," Colt told his cousin, returning the glare. "I don't want it."

Great-aunt Tillie was sitting in the buckboard only a few feet from where the two cousins faced off. "Colt never was the outlaw you are," she called now. "It's you your Uncle Travers would pick to lead the family."

"Poor little Colt was such a good boy, not a bit like his daddy," his grandmother's voice twittered, birdlike, from her perch beside Aunt Tillie on the wagon bench.

"All due respect, Old Aunties," Cyrus said to them. "Colt Wesson's got a blood obligation to lead us in crime. It's been so since Grandpappy Travers's day."

Colt Wesson had cut his baby teeth on the bitter taste of blood obligation. He'd have accepted that obligation if it hadn't involved robbing innocent folks of what they had worked hard to earn.

"My only obligation is to take Aunt Tillie and my grandmother away from here."

Hot wind blew a hank of hair into his eyes. He turned, then lifted his foot to step onto the buckboard.

A hand grabbed his collar, dragging him backward. From the corner of his vision he saw uncles and cousins leap off the porch and run toward the brewing fight.

Colt reached behind him, grabbed Cyrus's collar then bent over at the waist. His cousin flipped, landing in the dirt with a grunt.

Quicker than Colt could step away, Cyrus tripped him with a boot hook to the back of the knee.

He and his cousin rolled about in the dirt, toward the barn then the house. They exchanged a mouthful of cusswords before they each felt the crack of a cane on their backsides.

Aunt Tillie, having climbed down from her seat on the wagon, stood over them, poking the stick that she had never really needed for walking, in Cyrus's belly, then Colt's.

The two men broke apart, sitting on their rumps in the dirt like shamefaced children. Great-aunt Tillie had always been the peacemaker between brothers and cousins. Although she was now elderly, and they were grown men, it didn't make a difference.

"Cyrus," she said with a frown, "you will apologize to your cousin."

"Shouldn't have jumped you from behind," he mumbled. "Still doesn't change the fact that you ought to snatch a bride and bring her home, just the way it's always been done. Time you took your rightful place and made your pappy proud for once."

The last thing he intended to do was make the man who had named him after firearms proud.

Colt stood up warily. Cyrus did the same. They might have gone at each other again had Aunt Tillie's cane not been swinging.

"Colt," Great-aunt Tillie said, "you will apologize to your cousin for throwing him on the ground."

"I'm sorry for that, Cyrus." He wasn't, not a bit. His cousin would have been insulted had he reacted peacefully. But since Aunt Tillie set great store by a handshake, he stuck out his fist. "Just so you know, if the day comes that I do take a wife, I won't need to kidnap her…and I won't bring her here."

"Colty, dear," his grandmother said with a chuckle and a smile, "a lady does want a bit of romance. I was all aflutter when Grandpappy Travers tossed me across his saddle."

The real story was that she nearly shot him through the heart. But Colt wouldn't point that out to Grannie Rose, since she was fairly glowing with the inaccurate memory.

To his knowledge, the only woman to come willingly to the Broken Brand had been Great-aunt Tillie. She'd charged the ranch in the dead of night with a six-shooter blazing, intending to bring her sister home. The trouble was, by then Rose had fallen in love with Grandpappy.

Great-aunt Tillie had stayed on ever since, watching over Rose and teaching each new generation of children to read. For an ignorant outlaw gang, the Traverses were well-read.

"Come on." He took his trim, straight-backed great-aunt by the elbow. "It's time to go."

"It was time fifty-six years ago," she stated with a glare at the assembled Traverses. "Whichever one of you that takes over better make sure the children don't run wild. Make them learn their letters."

Colt lifted Aunt Tillie onto the buckboard seat even though she could have climbed up on her own. Seventy-six years looked easy on her.

He climbed up after her, picked up the reins then clicked to the horses.

He drove a slow circle about the yard while Aunt Tillie scowled at one and all and Grannie Rose blew kisses.

Colt hoped he was doing the right thing by taking the women from the only home they had known for most of their lives, but, damn it…the place was barely fit for pigs.

"You'll rue the day, Colt Wesson!" he heard Cyrus call out behind him. "A man can't set aside his kin!"

Holly Jane Munroe sat at a lace-covered table and stared out the window of her shop, The Sweet Treat. Balancing a knife in her fingers, she whirled a curlicue on the top of the cake she was frosting without even having to look at it.

She sighed and wished that Billy Folsom wasn't standing in front of the bank, staring back at her. He twirled his hat in his fingers, brushed a strand of curly hair from his forehead then tugged the tips of his heavy black mustache.

With an inhalation big enough to be noticeable from across the road, he stepped off the boardwalk. The poor fellow looked nervous; clearly buying a sweet treat was not the first thought on his mind.

There was nothing to be done about it, then, but to hurry behind the counter, setting row upon row of cookies, chocolates and pies between them.

And smile—she owed her swain that much, since he likely didn't want to be ringing the tinkling bell over her front door any more than she wanted him to be.

"Good afternoon, Billy." She hoped the smile would conceal her feeling that the sooner he was gone the better.

Billy was handsome…he was young. At twenty-one years old he was only two years her junior. The Folsoms had sent far worse her way over the past few months.

"Miss Holly Jane," he stated with a nod of his head. He wiped his damp brow with his sleeve. "I've come to… Well, that is, I'm here to—"

Billy crushed his hat in both of his fists. He inhaled a huge lungful of air.

"Will you marry me, Holly Jane?"

"I'm sorry, Billy, but no." It was hard to miss the relief that darted across his expression. "Please tell your grandfather that I have no intention of marrying anyone. Besides, what do you expect Lettie Coulter would have to say about that?"

Lettie and Billy had been sweet on each other since fourth grade.

"Thank you for the turndown, Holly Jane." He crammed his mangled hat on his head, grinning. "Pa's going to be put out some…again."

"Take this with you." Holly Jane handed him the cake she had just frosted. "That might sweeten him up some."

"Might, but only for a while." Billy stretched across the counter and kissed her cheek. "Be careful, Holly Jane. I spotted a Broadhower two blocks away."

"I'll be safe enough. You might want to go out my back door, though."

"Much obliged."

Billy glanced out the front window then hurried out the back door.

Holly Jane watched him trot down the path that passed through the oak grove behind the shop. With fall a week old, the leaves had begun to show some color. This evening, she hoped the walk home would be pretty enough to wipe her mind clean of troubles.

And thinking of trouble, it had been avoided by only seconds. The instant that she closed the back door on Billy, Henry Broadhower stormed in, red-faced and breathing hard.

"Good day, Henry." Henry was close to thirty years old and already beginning to lose his hair. His round belly rose and fell with his breathing. "I said no to Billy, if that's what's got you riled."

"Would have got me riled, but looks like you've got some common sense, for a frilly girl."

She smiled at him because it was the easiest way to deal with the man. "What's wrong with a frilly girl? Sugar and spice makes for a more pleasant town, don't you whink."

"Having no Folsoms in it would make it a better place."

"Say what you came to, Henry," she said with a sigh. In her opinion the town would be better off without a Folsom or a Broadhower to spread animosity. Their feud had caused tension for as long as she could remember.

"I'd be pleased if you'd become my wife, Miss Holly Jane."

"I'm sorry, Henry, but no." Even a frilly girl set her hopes higher than marrying to settle a feud.

When the color began to rise in his face once more, she plucked a cake from the case, apples and cream by heavens, and set it in his hands.

"Give your family my regards," she said, walking to the front door. Henry passed through it, slump-shouldered and grumbling.

Mercy me! She plucked a square of chocolate

from a display dish and popped it in her mouth. It melted over her tongue, sweet and smooth.

If the day presented one more proposal, she wouldn't make a single dollar.

"My word, isn't this a lovely town?" Sitting beside Colt on the buggy bench, Aunt Tillie patted his knee. "I believe this will be the home I've dreamed of all my life. See how the trees are begging to turn for the fall. I truly missed trees back at the Broken Brand."

His great-aunt was right. The green hill country of Texas looked like heaven compared to the desolate badlands of Nebraska.

"Friendship Springs," Grannie Rose read the sign announcing the name of the town. "I reckon it's full of friendly folks, don't you?"

Many of them would be friendly, but Colt knew that there was a feud dividing two of the old-time families and he was landing himself right in the middle of it.

"Hell, Grannie Rose," he said, "we'll be happy as three butterflies in a meadow."

"Colt Travers, what have I told you about that language?" Aunt Tillie swatted his hand where the reins lay lightly in his fingers.

"Don't use it." He winked at her and earned a frown, but it wasn't genuine. His great-aunt had doted on him from the moment he bawled his first lungful of air.

He'd try and be more careful with his language, but he'd worked the railroad for eleven years, dealing with rough men and stubborn locomotives, and his manners had turned coarse. The only thing guaranteed to bring on foul language quicker than a Travers relative was a damn, stubborn steam engine fighting his efforts to repair it.

Today, all that was behind him. He'd bought himself a ranch, sight unseen, just outside Friendship Springs. The seller had been a stranger who had become a friend over dinner and a beer. He never doubted the old man when he said the ranch looked like it had slipped through a hole in paradise and landed in Texas. It would provide wide green pastures for his horses and a snug home for the old ladies.

He wouldn't let the fact that his ranch was bordered by the two feuding families—the Folsoms to the west and the Broadhowers to the south—bother him. He'd grown up with trouble most of his life.

"Lordy, will you look at that?" Aunt Tillie exclaimed, pointing toward Town Square.

Town Square was not a square but a circle with a clear bubbling spring at its center. It looked to be a gathering place, since it had benches and flowerpots all about. Pleasant-looking stores surrounded the square. He'd make sure to bring Grannie Rose and Aunt Tillie back here for some shopping and visiting with friendly folks. That's not something they had done in the past, being shut away at the Broken Brand most of their lives.

"There's a shop that says The Sweet Treat," Grannie Rose exclaimed, nearly trembling with excitement. "It's been an age since I had a sweet treat that I didn't make for myself and a dozen others."

"Past time you did, then, Grannie," Colt answered. A sweet treat sounded just the thing before he settled the women into the hotel for the evening. They could set off for the ranch in the morning, fresh and rested.

Had it only been him traveling, he'd have been settled at the ranch weeks ago, but the old women had required a gentler pace.

Three doors down from the sweet shop he drew the buggy horses up sharp when a rolling ruckus broke out in front of them.

Two men lunged at each other, poking with balled-up fists and kicking at each other's tender spot. Neither of the fools knew how to fight. They were just as likely to drown in the spring as to do the other in.

"Hand me my cane, Colt," Aunt Tillie ordered after the men careened into a flowerpot and sent the orange mums flying.

"Let them be. It's none of our concern… Besides the fools will give it up before anyone's taken hard damage."

One man got the better of his enemy and pinned him to the ground. The fellow on top balled his fist, aimed for the grounded man's nose. Too bad for him that the combatant on the bottom turned his head. The balled fist slammed into dirt as hard as a rock.

A holler of pain shot about Friendship Spring's spring.

"Ain't no yellow-bellied, low-moraled Folsom going to wed Holly Jane," one of them shouted.

"Any Broadhower puts a ring on her finger's going to feel my bullet in his back!"

Colt grunted in disgust. With talk of a gun, things had taken a dangerous turn. Any rattlehead could kill from a distance.

Now, with the mention of Miss Holly Jane, things had suddenly become his business.

The only reason William Munroe had sold him the ranch was to keep his granddaughter from falling prey to the feud between the families. Had he left the land to the spinster, she would have become a pawn in the Folsoms' and the Broadhowers' lust for her property.

Through that prime ground flowed the river that fed water to the Folsom spread on the west and the Broadhower spread on the south.

Whoever controlled the water controlled their enemy.

Apparently, old William Munroe had been rightly worried about his granddaughter.

This was as good a time as any to set matters right. Colt drew his long, double-bladed knife from the sheath slung across his back. He let the weight of the Arkansas Toothpick balance across his palm, while he chose his target.

Since Broadhower stood up, he was it.

Colt watched the man's boot twitch. If he didn't get out of the way, Folsom would be caught between the boot and the back of a bench. It looked like Broadhower meant to crush a rib or two.

Colt threw the knife. The hiss of cold, sharp steel cut the air, barely disturbing the fair afternoon.

Broadhower gasped when he found his pant leg suddenly pinned to the bench.

Colt jumped from the buggy and strode slowly toward Broadhower, who glanced ogle-eyed at him, then the knife.

Colt plucked the blade from the bench, yanking it from his pant leg.

He glared at Broadhower, then at Folsom. "From now on, Saphead…and you, Featherbrain, Miss Munroe is off-limits."

"Says who?" Folsom and Broadhower spoke together.

"Says the new owner of the Munroe place."

In the face of a shocked expression and a furious one, Colt climbed back into the buggy and settled between the ladies.

"You boys have a nice day." He flashed them a smug grin that was sure to make them steam.

"Why, will you look at that?" Grannie craned her neck to look behind as he led the team toward the bakery. "There's mashed cake spread all over town square."

* * *

Colt watched Grannie Rose's grin crinkle while she sighed over each and every sweet treat in the display case. The three-week trip from the Broken Brand to Friendship Springs had been worth it for this moment alone.

Grannie's mind wasn't as clear as it had once been. Now and then she saw things that weren't there. Still and all, she was his grandmother, and he meant to see that she enjoyed every year that she had left.

"I'll take one of everything, except those chocolate hearts," Grannie announced, and clapped her hands. "I'll take two of those."

"You'll take two sweets and one chocolate heart," Aunt Tillie said in the tone that she used on contrary toddlers.

Looked like his spoiling of Grannie might have to be done on the sly.

"Oh, Tillie, you need to loosen your corset strings on occasion." Grannie nudged her sister in the ribs.

At that moment the curtain to the back room rustled and a young woman stepped through. For half a second he was stunned by her resemblance to a heavenly angel.

"Good afternoon," she said, gazing at him with eyes as rich a brown as the fancy chocolates piled on the plate between them. "How can I help you?"

With a sugar sweet kiss was the first thought to

pop into his mind, but clearly, this was not the kind of woman that a man casually canoodled.

"I'll have one of everything," Grannie Rose declared. "Except for the hearts, I'll have three of those...and so will my sister."

"Make yourself sick then, but don't think I'll be up all night caring for you," Aunt Tillie huffed.

The woman smiled at Grannie, then Aunt Tillie. Hell if she didn't look as sweet as the pastries covering the counter.

"May I make a suggestion?" she asked.

"Anything that will keep my sister from the sin of gluttony."

"I'll take your suggestion, dearie," Grannie said. "As long as it comes with four hearts of chocolate."

"As a matter of fact, it comes with a plateful of them to share among you. I guarantee no one will become sick from it."

Colt tried not to stare at her, but the woman was damned pretty. He'd seen a pink rose once that was a match to the blush in her cheeks.

"As long as it's not the whole contents of the display case, we'll take it," Aunt Tillie said.

"Just have a seat at the table over there by the window. Won't take but a minute to prepare."

Fresh is what best described her...fresh and luminous. He'd never seen a luminous woman before, but just to prove his thought, when she walked through a beam of afternoon sunshine streaking through a window on her way to the back room, her blond hair turned gold, like the light was inside it.

He didn't realize that he had been staring calf-eyed at the curtain until Aunt Tillie asked if he was ailing.

He shook his head. "Just a mite wearied from the trip."

"She's a very pretty young lady." Grannie studied him with a look. She arched a fine gray brow. "In fact, Colt Wesson, I believe she is the one for you."

Aunt Tillie rolled her eyes and shrugged.

"Grannie, she's not my kind of woman at all. I'm partial to the earthy kind."

Once again Aunt Tillie rolled her eyes. This time she sighed out loud.

That's right, earthy with a whiff of sin about them.

Hell, he wasn't her kind of man. She would require a gentleman.

It threw him off a bit when, a few moments later, the angel emerged from the back room and a surge of desire rocked him to his dusty boots.

She glided toward them with a tray balanced on her palm set with daintily painted teacups and a plate of chocolates. The scent of cinnamon, mint and cloves rose from the delicate china.

"There's a dash of everything in the tea, and it won't do a bit of harm to ladylike figures," she said, placing the teacups on the lace tablecloth then setting the plate of chocolates in the middle.

Grannie Rose caught her hand before she walked away. "You are a lovely girl. Not married, I hope."

"No, ma'am." Colt didn't miss the shadow that passed over her soft brown eyes.

Grannie winked at him.

He was in for it now. Once Grannie Rose had a notion about something it was difficult to dissuade her from it.

Next trip to The Sweet Treat, he'd wait outside. He'd take a peek or two through the window, but what man wouldn't?

"There's a pig nibbling on my boot toe," Grannie Rose announced.

"Really, Rose," Aunt Tillie whispered. "Don't insult the proprietor by saying such a ridiculous thing."

"But there is a pig, a small one, but a pig, nonetheless, and it's nipping my footwear."

Colt glanced at the lovely shop owner to see if the lady meant to kick them out over Grannie's words. Her cheeks were flushed...turning redder by the second.

"Apologize, Rose!" Aunt Tillie had turned nearly as red as the angel, who swished her yellow skirt rounding the pastry counter.

"Look for yourself, then." Grannie lifted the table lace.

"Lulu!" The angel dashed forward.

By damn, it was a pig! A pig with a pink ribbon tied through a slot in its ear. It was hard to know what surprised him more, the presence of the pig or that he had failed to notice it under the table. But Grannie was right. It was a very little pig.

The angel rushed for the pig; the pig dashed from under the table snagging the lace tablecloth around its foot.

Tea and chocolate went sailing, while fragile cups hit the floor and shattered. He caught a blue one and saved it.

He and the old ladies jumped up and backed away from the table a heartbeat before the pig ran into the leg and knocked it over with a smash and clatter.

Aunt Tillie laughed out loud. The animal squealed while the angel dashed here and there in pursuit of it.

The pig collided with Colt's shin then skidded across the floor in a mess of hot tea and melting chocolate. He lunged for it with one hand because he gripped the surviving teacup in the other. The smooth round belly of the creature passed through his grip like it had been buttered. It spun in a circle on short legs then made a dash between Colt's feet.

"Lulu!" the angel screeched.

She ran forward, stepped in a square of slick chocolate then slipped, sliding belly first…between his legs.

By now Aunt Tillie was laughing so hard that she began to wheeze.

By a bit of good luck, the pig tangled itself in Grannie's skirt. Colt grabbed it by the scruff while the angel slowly rose to her feet.

She wouldn't know it, glowering at the animal like she was, but her belly was streaked in chocolate. Even better, chocolate rings circled each of her breasts, revealing that they were plump...womanly.

"Here's your bacon." He stuffed the squealing, wriggling creature under her arm then handed her the blue teacup.

"Blast it, Lulu," she muttered, then looked up with a furious blush staining her cheeks. "I beg your pardon, sir...ladies. Please do come another day for tea and chocolate...on the house naturally."

She spun about then disappeared behind the curtain, the piglet's tail twitching with the scolding it was getting.

"I do have to say, Colt," Aunt Tillie managed to say while attempting to bring her laughter under control, "the girl is a bit earthy."

"I knew she was the one for you the moment I saw her, Colty."

"Hell," he grumbled, and his aunt didn't even bother to frown.

Chapter Two

"I should have let the butcher keep you," Holly Jane grumbled at the pig, who grunted at a weed growing near the back door of The Sweet Treat. "You'd have made a fine sandwich."

She locked the door then glanced about. So far, not a single suitor was visible on the path through the woods that led home.

That, at least, was a blessing. With the sun dipping behind the treetops, she didn't need another delay. She would be late getting back to the ranch as it was.

What with broken china scattered about and chocolate-tea goop to be scrubbed from the floor, it was well past the time that she liked to be home.

"You, Miss Pigling, will help me feed the chickens since they'll be cackling up a storm by time we get to the barn."

Holly Jane walked the path toward home taking

deep breaths of autumn-scented air. Late-afternoon sunshine shot through tree branches and cast long shadows behind her and Lulu. Leaves twisted in the breeze, looking like molten gold and then red sparks.

She loved her life here. When she had discovered, at the reading of his will, that Granddaddy had sold her inheritance, she had cried for a week. Between missing the man who had been everything to her and wondering how she would get by without the ranch she had planted her roots in, she thought she might never quit weeping.

Overhead, a crow cawed, flapping its wings toward the west and the coming sunset.

Given a choice, Holly Jane would be snuggled in a cozy chair beside the fireplace when darkness came. Since she didn't have the choice, she would make another one. She would enjoy the beauty of the evening as it faded from light to dusk then full dark.

Coming out of the woods just now, she watched the sun slip behind the trees growing on the western edge of the ranch. The great orange glow peeked between a line of cedar and cottonwood, with elm and maple tossed in.

It would be dark by the time she reached the house, but a fat full moon rose behind her to light the way. Stars began to blink and twinkle. A raccoon rustled out of the brush and waddled up to Lulu.

"Good evening, Mayberry."

Lulu oinked and the pair of them toddled behind

Holly Jane toward the ranch house…the home she couldn't even think of leaving.

Blame it, she wouldn't leave. She had vowed that, to herself if to no one else.

Grandfather, in his wisdom…or confusion… hadn't sold the entire ranch to the stranger. He had left her a perfect circle of land a hundred yards in diameter and only a short distance from the house.

Smack in the middle of the circle of land was her carousel, the gift Granddaddy had given her when she was five years old.

Why hadn't he left her the house, as well? What could it have hurt to do that? These questions had plagued her like hounds on a scent.

Her grandfather had meant well, the lawyer had explained that day when her tears wouldn't stop. Granddaddy's intention had been to keep her from falling prey to the Folsoms and the Broadhowers, who would do anything to get the Munroe land.

"The new owner has agreed to watch over you, Holly Jane," the lawyer had explained. "Your grand-daddy only wanted to keep you safe."

Holly Jane stepped onto the bridge that crossed the narrow river that Granddaddy had named Neigh-borly Creek. She sighed so deep that it must have alarmed Mayberry. The racoon stood on her back legs with her paws scratching the air.

"Can't think of what got into Granddaddy. I don't need a stranger looking after me. Haven't I been watching after him and me since Grandma passed?"

Lulu oinked then trotted over the bridge. Holly Jane hurried after her. The chickens were probably pecking each other by now.

Two hours later, Holly Jane sat down on an over-stuffed chair beside the fireplace with a cup of hot cocoa warming her palms.

The house looked like it had been shaken about in a jug then the contents dropped like gambling dice to lie where they landed.

Until Granddaddy's passing, she had kept these rooms swept and in order. She'd put flowers in vases on the dining room table. She'd let fresh air waft in through open widows, carrying the scent of summer blossoms through the house.

But summer was gone and so was Granddaddy. And the stranger was on his way. As much as it hurt to turn the house she loved into a tumbleweed, she did not want the new owner to see it at its best. If she could prevent him from falling in love with the place, it would be easier for him to sell it back to her.

After a while, she couldn't bear the unkempt look of the rooms so she went outside.

Her carousel glowed dully in the moonlight. She hugged her robe around her white nightgown, went down the steps and walked over newly deeded Travers land to her own inherited circle.

She stepped upon the carousel platform. It creaked, showing its age. She ran her hand over the peeling red paint of a horse's rump.

There had been a day when the carousel still

worked—before the steam engine that powered it quit—that she would ride for hours on end. Even the children from town would come to the ranch on Sunday afternoons. As hard as it was to believe, for those hours, the Folsom children and the Broadhower children forgot the feud between their parents and played peacefully together.

Holly Jane climbed onto the back of her favorite wooden horse. She glanced at the sky. An owl beat silently against the dark, its pale wings bright against the canopy of stars. It screeched and a mouse exploring the platform dashed between the boards to safety.

Years had gone by since those days; the carousel had broken and faded. The children had grown up to hate each other.

"I understand why you sold the ranch, Granddaddy," she whispered to miles of shadowed land, quiet except for the scurrying night creatures.

And she forgave him. She only hoped that from wherever he was, he could see that she had avoided becoming a Mrs. to a Broadhower or a Folsom and she'd done it all on her own.

When she did become a Mrs., it would be because she was madly and completely head over heels in love with some handsome man who was brave, tender and devoted all at once.

To her knowledge, that man did not exist in Friendship Springs. From what she had seen of men, he might not exist at all.

Holly Jane gripped the carousel pole and leaned her cheek against it.

Then again, he may have passed through this afternoon, and thanks to Lulu, seen her at her very worst. She had cursed, blame it, right in front of him and the old ladies.

Oh well, chances are he was only passing through. But he was handsome...so handsome that it was hard to put him out of her mind.

He had sandy, brown-blond hair that grew past the collar of his flannel shirt and the shadow of a beard. It could be that he might have forgotten to shave...or maybe he was beginning to grow it out.

A body wouldn't think she'd had time to notice his eyes, but lordy, they were blue and they flickered mischief. She didn't know him well enough... she didn't know him at all, really...to know this to be true, but she'd lay a bet on it.

And honestly, the pair of dimples flashing in his stubble-roughened cheeks when he had handed her Lulu and called her *bacon* had nearly made her fall again.

As far as handsome went in her requirement of a husband, the stranger was all that and more.

Still, there was brave, tender and devoted to be considered. Chances are he was devoted, having taken his valuable time to bring a pair of old women to tea.

Whether he would be brave and tender in a marriage, she had no way of knowing. He might be mar ried already. She ought to quit daydreaming and recognize that.

And aside from everything else, there was one more quality she would require of a mate. He would have to be a good kisser. Over the years she had imagined kisses of all kinds. Tender, wild, demanding and sweet as sugar.

There was one thing she did know about the stranger. Fate would never give her the opportunity to discover what mysteries those expressive lips might hold.

It was nearly dawn and Holly Jane hadn't managed to capture a wink of sleep. There was something wrong with her bed and she knew just what it was.

It was no longer her bed. After years of snuggling into its downy sweetness, it was now the property of one Colt Travers. Every feather of her mattress and each neatly fluffed bow on her quilt belonged to him.

She threw back the covers and sat up. She set her bare feet on the cool floorboards and shivered for a moment.

"Get off my robe, Lulu." She poked the pig with her toe, then picked up her robe and put it on.

Thoughts of a stranger coming into her home were unsettling. He'd walk about the rooms that she loved without knowing that Grandma had set pies in the kitchen window to cool, that Granddaddy smoked a pipe while he sat on the step of the front porch. He wouldn't know that her mama walked out the front door with a sideshow barker while Holly Jane slept upstairs and that she had never come back. He wouldn't know that the photo on the mantel was of her father and that he had died in a fire before she was born.

To Holly Jane, the stranger would feel the same as a thief. He'd invade her home and take everything familiar. He'd replace it with his own belongings and leave her bereft.

Colt Travers would do that, if she let him.

"Come on, Lulu, wouldn't you like to nibble something in the parlor?"

The rooster crowed in the barn. Soon another day would begin and there was still no sign of the new owner. No doubt he was taking his own good time, not caring that her stomach ached with the suspense of waiting for the unknown.

She gathered courage coming down the stairs, by reminding herself that she wasn't helpless. She had her weapons, although she hated to use them.

Her first stop was the dining room. A vase of dried-out flowers sat in the middle of the table. She tipped them over, broke a brittle stem and then wiped up a smear of water with the hem of her robe. She didn't want to do permanent damage to the table. It would be hers again one day if the new owner didn't sell it and put something repulsive in its place.

She ripped a cushion on the divan that was worn and needed replacing anyway. She scattered a handful of stuffing about the floor, which delighted Lulu to no end. The petite pig snorted at it and pushed it about with her snout.

After half an hour, the ruination of the house was satisfactory and she became weary. Just one more thing would make it a work of art.

"Come along, Lulu," she called and walked into the kitchen.

She picked up a cookie from a plate that she had left on the table more than a week ago. It had aged to dry, crumbly perfection.

Holly Jane closed her fist about it and scattered crumbs of cinnamon and nutmeg over the table. She sprinkled some on the floor. The crumbs on the floor didn't last because of Lulu.

Next, she went to the pantry and took out a bag of flour.

"All right, Lulu, give it your best." She scattered the flour on the countertop and the stove. Then she tossed a handful in the air and let it land where it would.

"Almost perfect," she muttered then dumped the rest of the bag on the floor.

Lulu squealed then rolled in it. She was a strange little creature. Most pigs enjoyed a roll in the mud. Not so her little friend—she liked wearing pretty bows in her ear and eating sweets.

"Go on now," she said to the pig. "Trot about the house. Leave prints wherever you can."

Lulu squinted small piggy eyes at her and lifted her flour-smeared snout.

"I won't get angry. I promise."

Lulu paddled into the parlor, happily grunting.

At last, fatigue weighted every muscle of Holly Jane's body. She climbed the staircase toward the bed that used to be hers, thankful that this was Sunday. The Sweet Treat would be closed, and she would be able to sleep past sunup.

She fell into bed with flour caking her toes, smudging her nose and frosting her hair, but she was too weary to worry about it. She might sleep through Lulu's demand for breakfast, and the little pig could be as persistent as an itch.

"Did you remember the parasol, Colt?" Grannie Rose asked while Colt lifted her onto the wagon seat. "And my blue satin dancing slippers?"

"Tucked away between your bloomers and your new straw bonnet." At least the parasol was. The dancing slippers had gone to dust thirty years before.

Colt climbed up and settled between his grannie and his great-aunt. He felt the solid weight of the bench beneath him and inhaled the scent of new lumber.

He'd purchased the spanking new wagon after the old ladies had been tucked into the hotel, each with a glass of wine.

Excitement over seeing his new spread had kept him awake all night, so he'd risen before dawn to load the few belongings that had come with them from the Broken Brand and the trinkets that the ladies had taken a fancy to along the way.

They wouldn't need much in the way of home goods since the ranch house had come with all the furnishings. He'd buy everything new for the barn, though. He meant to pamper the horses he would be breeding like they were kin…maybe not his own, but someone's.

Ever since he'd been a kid he'd dreamed of having land where the strong beautiful creatures would run and frolic. Horses weren't like cattle that were raised for the slaughterhouse. His animals would go for farming, pulling buggies, or the high-spirited ones might even go for racing.

Horses might have been what convinced William Munroe to sell him the land. He'd said that his granddaughter would be knee-deep in pleasure over it.

Evidently, Holly Jane had some sort of kinship with critters.

"Let's get going, Colt," Aunt Tillie said, nudging him in the ribs. "Woolgathering won't get us to our new home."

"Poor little Holly Jane must be frightened out there all by herself," Grannie Rose said.

"She ain't little, Grannie." For some reason, Grannie thought Holly Jane was a child, even though he'd told her that she wasn't, time and again. "She's a spinster lady."

"Is she?" Grannie frowned then brightened. "She ought to get on fine with Tillie, then."

He hoped so. The care of three females, one not related, might be a challenge. He couldn't imagine that the spinster would be grateful to see him, even though he was there to stand between her and the fool, feuding families.

The ride from town to the ranch was short. Only fifteen minutes by wagon…five, he figured, on horseback.

While the old ladies chatted, he watched the scenery pass and thought of William Munroe.

It had been nothing short of Providence, the pair of them meeting and becoming friends in so short a time.

The old man had been away from home on personal business having to do with his health, and was trying to get home but the locomotive of the train he had been traveling on had gone sour in a town called Presley Wells. Colt had been called to repair it. It had taken a few days and lodging was scarce. Colt and the old man shared a room and the stories of their lives.

All at once, the woods ended and the ranch came into view.

"Oh my, Colt," Aunt Tillie said. "This is beautiful. Just what you dreamed of."

It took some self-control not to leap from the

bench and shout. In his mind he saw his horses running free with their tails and manes flying behind them.

"I'd like a ride on that carousel." Grannie clapped her hands, her smile beaming.

"Really, Rose you know there's no carousel way out here."

A crow circled overhead, cawing.

"I may be losing my mind, Tillie, but you've lost your eyesight."

"There is a carousel, Aunt Tillie." Colt pointed to the spot where the faded machine sat a few hundred yards from the house.

The small plot of ground that held the carousel was Holly Jane's land.

He wondered if she was bitter at the loss of the ranch. He hoped not. Could be, she felt freed of a burden.

At any rate, he hoped that the woman, likely getting past her prime and giving up on hope of a husband, would fit in well with Grannie Rose and Aunt Tillie. As part of the land deal, he'd agreed to let Holly Jane live in the house and to watch over her.

They crossed the bridge over the pretty, clear flowing river called Neighborly Creek. In a few more minutes he drew the horses to a halt in front of the house.

"Welcome home, ladies," Colt said, wondering if either of them had noticed the hitch in his voice.

The place welcomed him before he ever walked

in the front door. The porch wrapped all the way around the house so that a body could stand on it facing east and see the sunrise in the morning then sit on a chair facing west and watch the sun go down behind the grove of trees at the western edge of the property.

Thanks, old man, Colt thought, and hoped William knew how sorry he was for the circumstances that made Colt the new owner.

He helped Grannie and Aunt Tillie from the wagon. With a hand under each of their arms he escorted them to their new front door.

Comparing this home to the one they had left behind was like comparing a fistful of spring flowers to a tumbleweed.

He reached for the doorknob.

"I believe it's only right for us to knock," Aunt Tillie said. "Miss Holly Jane might take a fright to see strangers walking into her house."

He sincerely hoped he wasn't inheriting a frail and skittish female. Heaven help him, he could almost see her now, a pinch-faced old biddy too shy to find a man…and looking dried-out as straw.

But he'd given his word to watch out for her, and he would. He'd care for her the same as he would Grannie Rose or Aunt Tillie.

He knocked on the door, not too loud, in case the poor woman was the nervous kind.

No answer. He knocked again, louder. With still no answer, he opened the door.

The three of them stepped inside.

"Oh, my word," Aunt Tillie whispered. "It looks like a whirly wind passed through."

"I do hope the poor little dear hasn't been carried off by a Folsom," Grannie said, her voice cracking in alarm.

"Or a Broadhower." Aunt Tillie touched her throat with a delicate age-spotted hand.

He'd place his bet on the former lady of the house being none too pleased to give it up. Chances are she wasn't waiting with a tea-and-scone welcome.

Colt led the way through the dining room, where dried-out posies lay scattered on the table, then to the kitchen, where it looked like a pastry explosion had occurred.

Small human footprints tracked through a dusting of flour on the floor, along with some four-legged prints that looked suspiciously piglike.

It couldn't be, but how many times had he seen an oinker indoors? Only once, and that was yesterday.

He left the kitchen and made a right for the stairs with the old ladies close behind him. There was a heavy feeling in his gut that his charge might not be the retiring violet he had imagined.

She might be temptation dressed in an angel's guise.

He opened the first closed door he came to.

Hell and damn. Curled smack in the middle of the bed was a miniature pig flicking its ear so that the pink bow tied in it looked like a waving hankie.

Curled up about the pig was yesterday's angel covered in the proof of her crime and not a whole lot else.

Flour dusted her cheeks and dappled her hair. One hand lay against the pillow, dainty fingers curled, the other under her pink cheek. Her lips puckered in her sleep, looking soft and moist.

"I told you she was the one, Colt." Grannie Rose bent over the bed, peering at Miss Holly Jane. "If she wasn't, she wouldn't look so at home in your bed."

Chapter Three

"The reason she looks at home is because she is." Holly Jane heard a man's voice say, the tone so rich it made her imagine melted caramel.

She snuggled more deeply into her dream, trying to savor the sound. It was a shame that she couldn't see him, but he had popped into the dream without warning. His voice was a welcome change from the stubborn suitor she was trying to send on his way... and something burning in the oven at the kitchen of The Sweet Treat.

No wonder it was burning if she had been so careless as to return home without taking whatever was baking out of the oven. Just then the dream fog cleared from her brain. Nothing was burning. She was home in her bed.

She sighed deeply, snuggling into the pillow and wishing she might return to the dream. She would face the stubborn suitor and the ruined baked goods in order to hear that other manly voice one more time.

"Wake up, Mischief Muffin."

Her eyes popped open before her vision cleared. Peering down at her was the blurred face of the man she had spun castle's in the air about last night. The man whose voice had trespassed into her dream.

The man that Lulu had humiliated her in front of!

He gazed down at her with a grin and eyes bluer than any she had ever seen…and a pair of dimples that very clearly knew what deviltry was all about.

Disturbingly, her first reaction to him was not "What are you doing in my bedroom?" or "Get off my property!" but "I think I'm in love."

Which was impossible, because one didn't fall in love willy-nilly with a stranger bending over one's bed. One would screech and scratch until he ran away.

"You always sleep with a pig, Bo Peep?"

Suddenly, her senses snapped back into place.

"I never sleep with—" The weight of the bed shifted near her belly. "Lulu!"

She pushed at Lulu's rump. Hopping off the bed with a grunt, she hit the floor in a puff of flour.

Holly Jane sat up, grabbed her robe from the spindle of the headboard then yanked her arms though the sleeves. She stood up.

Being a good head taller than she was, the man stared down at her. He was trouble for sure, with a gaze that threatened devilment even more than the dimples did.

What was he doing here? And the pair of elderly women with him? He couldn't be... Oh, please don't let him be—

She shivered, but only because the floorboards were cold under her bare feet.

"Come along, sister," a woman said. This was Grannie Rose, she recalled from yesterday afternoon's disaster. "Let's let the lovebirds get acquainted."

"They aren't lovebirds, Rose." The tall, slender woman led the shorter, rounder woman by the elbow. "By the looks of the house she's not well pleased to have any of us here."

And who would be pleased to be awoken from a sweet and spicy dream by trespassers...or so she desperately hoped.

"I'm sure that's not true, sister." Rose glanced back at her with a smile. "Miss Munroe is nearly kin."

The ladies walked out of the room.

The man stood too close, looking down with his dimples flaring and his lips... Well, she had to look away from them. Even though he remained silent, the creases at the corners of his eyes crinkled with laughter.

The chill in her toes shot goose bumps up her legs.

"Pleasure to meet you, Holly Jane."

The man, who she had by now decided could only be Mr. Colt Wesson Travers, tipped his head then backed out of the bedroom, clearly enjoying the fact that he had come upon her vulnerable and in her bed, wearing her nightgown—and sleeping with a pig to go with it.

Without warning, he winked, spun about on his boot heel and followed his elderly relatives down the stairs.

She had not by any means fallen instantly in love with this stranger! Just the opposite, she disliked him with a righteous intensity. He was arrogant… cocky…and much too handsome for anyone's good.

And he owned the ranch that should have been hers!

Half an hour later, Holly Jane stood at the top of the stairs, yanking the bow of her apron and listening to the murmur of voices drifting up the stairs.

The scent of fried potatoes drifted up as well, but she did her best to ignore it. One would think that the aroma would make her want to retch, being that a stranger was using her kitchen, but it only made her stomach growl.

With a sigh, she straightened her spine, the one in her back and the one in her soul. She descended the stairs determined to present the new owners with a smile. She would pass through the kitchen as quickly as possible on her way to her own circle of property, where she would make herself a cozy place to live.

No doubt that's what Granddaddy would have expected of her…a smile and a friendly greeting.

Blame it, her cheeks blushed like flames when she stepped into the kitchen and saw the three of them gathered about the dining table.

She'd like to blame the darn pig for it all, but it hadn't been Lulu's idea to ruin the house.

"Good morning," she said, and since they hadn't really been introduced and she could be anyone, she added. "I'm Holly Jane Munroe. Welcome home."

"Good morning, dear," the shorter woman said, her smile as agreeable as sunrise after a cold night. "I'm Grannie Rose, and this is my sister, Aunt Tillie. Our young man is my grandson, Colt Wesson."

"A pleasure," she said, nodding at each of the people sitting at the table because it was the polite thing to do and she was a polite person. "I'll be out of your way in a heartbeat."

"But we've saved you a chair," Grannie Rose said, sliding it away from the table for her to sit down.

"And a plate of food." Aunt Tillie pushed it toward the place they had saved for her.

"You must be hungry," Colt Travers said with a wink. "Working late…making the place ready."

"Colt Wesson, mind your manners." Aunt Tillie shot her nephew a frown.

"Please do eat with us, dear." Grannie Rose patted the chair seat. "You did a remarkable job on the house. I couldn't have sabotaged it better myself."

With her humiliation complete, Holly Jane felt her jaw drop open. It only took a second or two to recall her dignity, though. She straightened her shoulders and dug deep for the sunny smile she was noted for.

"Ordinarily, it's a lovely home," she said, then glanced about one more time, holding on to the vision of the curtains hanging at the kitchen window. Grandma had crocheted them only a month before the arthritis in her fingers became debilitating. She gazed at the table that Granddaddy had built with his own hands. If only she could sit at it one more time.

Since she just couldn't, she said the only thing to be said. "I hope you find joy here. I'll have my belongings out by noon."

Tears burned her eyes. She dashed out the kitchen door before anyone might notice them.

Daylight, warm and fresh with autumn, greeted her, but she would have to wait to savor it. As it was, she would barely make it to the carousel before she bawled her heart out.

Lulu, roused from her morning nap, waddled out from under the porch and followed on short pink legs.

Halfway to the carousel, she heard the chickens raising a fuss in the barn.

Blame it. She was late feeding them. Changing direction, she strode toward the barn, wiping her eyes with her apron.

She stopped and went suddenly still. The chickens were no longer hers. It wasn't her responsibility to feed them. If Mr. Colt Travers wanted his livestock fed he should have been here at dawn to do it.

Had the hens been merely livestock, she would have turned and gone back, left him to do his chore.

She probably shouldn't have, but over the years she had given every hen and rooster a name. She could hear Henrietta cackling with pride at the egg she must have just laid. And her sister Matilda was brooding a batch of eggs. The chicks were due to hatch in a week.

Holly Jane continued toward the barn. Once she knew that Colt Travers was competent in caring for the flock, she would allow him to take care of them.

All at once a sickening thought hit her like a blow to the belly. She stared at the house, watching through the window while three distant figures ate their breakfast.

What if the Travers family was partial to chicken and dumplings? What if their favorite Sunday dinner was fried chicken?

Today was Sunday!

She hurried to the barn trying to decide what to do. Feed the chickens, yes, but what then? Set them free to become prey to hawks? Keep them in their safe little yard where Colt Travers might make dinner of them?

For now she'd watch to see what the man had in mind. He would have to pass through her land to get

to the barn, or take a very long way around. She'd
know if he were up to no good.

After she fed the chickens, she turned her attention to the task at hand…creating her new home.
Over the past few weeks she had been collecting
things to fabricate a shelter under the dome of the
carousel. She had an oilcloth tarp to keep out the
wind and rain, a big bundle of blankets to fashion a
bed of, and two lanterns.

Last week, knowing that the new owners were
on the way, she had dragged a big trunk down from
the attic and stuffed it with corsets, petticoats, skirts
and blouses, aprons and gowns.

Only a few of her personal belongings remained
in the house. She ought to leave them there, spare
herself the pain and humiliation of going back inside, but they were some of her favorites.

Since there was no help for her situation but to
move on with life, Holly Jane picked up a hammer
and a big square nail. She began to tack her tarp to
the carousal poles.

As a child, she had begged Granddaddy to let her
live on the carousel. Well, here she was, her dream
fulfilled at last. Without a doubt, her grandfather
was somewhere in the Great Beyond having a good
belly laugh with Grandma.

Frowning, Colt stood on the front porch watching
Holly Jane trying to hammer a tarp to the carousel,

There were some things that needed setting straight, and he'd begin with breakfast.

The old man hadn't sold him the ranch with the expectation that his granddaughter would go hungry.

From the looks of things, she also planned to go cold. The temperature might be pleasant right now with the sun all warm and fuzzy, but once it set the night would turn blistering cold in a hurry.

He trotted down the steps with her breakfast plate, watching while she struggled with a hammer that was too heavy and a nail that was too big.

What did that little speck of a girl think she was going to do, live on the carousel?

That didn't fit with the vow he had made to her granddaddy. He was to care for the spinster...it was written in black and white right on the contract, as legal and binding as all the rest of it. Even if it weren't a legal obligation, he had given his word. He and William had shaken hands on it.

While it was clear that Holly Jane wasn't the dried prune that her grandfather had hinted at, he meant to live up to their agreement...and he meant to do it in the house.

He watched her struggle while he crossed the yard. One time she nearly had the tarp tacked up, but the wood was hard and the hammerhead slipped. The nail went flying.

The odd little pig scurried after it, her beribboned ear flapping.

"Don't you eat that, Lulu!" Holly Jane rucked up

her skirt and hurried down the short ladder she had been standing on.

"I never should have sneaked you out of the butcher's shed!" Holly Jane was so intent on chasing Lulu that she didn't even notice him coming toward her.

The pair of them wove in and out of wooden horses, fancy carved benches, a lion and an elephant.

Before he knew it, Colt was no longer frowning. Watching the pig's flapping bow and the woman's bouncing yellow skirt would turn the sourest day sweet.

But that's what Holly Jane specialized in, he reckoned, sugar and spice. He couldn't deny that watching the curvy figure of his charge romping about was a treat. He didn't even have to visit her shop in town to enjoy a sweet treat.

Too soon the chase ended and Holly Jane shot her pig a triumphant grin. She held the nail high with her delicate-looking fingers gripping it tight.

She climbed the short ladder, swinging yellow skirt and hammer in hand, clearly believing she would nail the tarp to the pole. Too bad the hammer was still too heavy and the nail too large.

The ladder began to wobble. Holly Jane dropped the hammer but held the tarp in place with her fingers.

He reached for the knife slung across his back and drew it from its sheath. He hoped Aunt Tillie was watching so she'd know how many uses his weapon had. She'd harped on him time and again to remove it at home. The trouble was, a man never knew when he might need its services.

Like right now.

Colt let the knife fly and watched with satisfaction as the blade pinned the tarp to the pole. And hell...there was even more satisfaction hearing Miss Sunbeam give a little screech.

She hopped off the ladder and glared at him.

"You could have cut my hand off!"

"Once we're better acquainted you'll know the blade was as good as a mile away."

He walked past her, picked up the hammer and plucked the nail from her fingers. Reaching over her head, he tacked the tarp to the pole with one blow then plucked his knife from the wood.

She tried to hide it, but Miss Holly Jane didn't seem pleased with his help. That was something she'd have to get used to since he was legally bound to provide it.

"We're neighbors and nothing more," she said. "I don't reckon I'll see all the things you can do with your blade."

The plate of food wobbled in his hand. While she blinked at him in virtuous innocence, he imagined all sorts of provocative images involving "his blade."

He was fairly certain that William Munroe had not meant for him to seduce his granddaughter.

Damn far from it… He was supposed to protect her from the advances of greedy suitors.

"Eat your breakfast, Holly Jane." He set the plate on the floor of the carousel.

She speared a glance at the cold food then at him. She plunked down on the creaky boards and set the plate in her lap. He sat down beside her.

"Look," he said, watching her nibble a biscuit, "I know you don't want us here. It must have been tough to find out your grandpappy had sold the place out from under you."

"I'll admit, I cried for a solid week." She looked at him with eyes the color of whiskey stirred in cocoa. "But you should know that I plan to buy it back from you as soon as I can."

"I ain't sellin', Sunshine." He was sorry that her dream had died with her grandfather, but his had only begun. "But you've got a home here as long as you want it."

"I have a carousel for a home. You, Mr. Travers, are a guest on my front porch."

"There's things worse than a carousel to inherit." A family of criminals, for one. "All that your grandfather wanted was for you to be safe. He knew the Folsoms and the Broadhowers would be after you, so he sold the land to me. Your circle of land being smack in the center of my ranch, guarantees that."

"I believe that we need to set down some neighborly rules." Holly Jane put down her plate after eating only the biscuit. "I need to pass through your land to go to town. You need to pass through my land to get to the barn. We should agree to allow that."

"I appreciate that. You walk freely over my land and I'll walk freely over yours."

"Not freely, but to and from. I'll keep to myself and you keep to yourself."

"Grannie Rose and Aunt Tillie have their hearts set on mothering you." She wanted that. He saw the need cross her expression like a ripple on water. "Come back to the house, Holly Jane."

"I'll stay on my own land, thank you very much."

She stood up, clearly dismissing him and his invitation.

"We're knee-deep in October. It'll be cold as hell tonight."

"Don't worry. Granddaddy built your house to be snug and warm."

She turned her back on him. Hell and damn… Nothing he said to the woman would make any difference.

She picked up her hammer and another nail.

He wouldn't help her this time. When she got cold enough she'd come inside.

At midnight, Holly Jane wrapped the tarp about her body and watched smoke rise from the chimney of the house. The imagined warmth inside made her shiver even more.

The wind had begun to howl at sundown and

picked up velocity ever since. Lulu had felt no shame in squealing outside the kitchen door until Grannie Rose let her in.

The little traitor had gone inside gleefully and was, no doubt, warm and coddled by now. At least the raccoon, Mayberry, hadn't deserted her. The sweet creature sat beside her, no doubt wondering what the foolish human was doing sitting out after dark in the cold.

Defying Granddaddy's wishes is what.

Colt Travers might believe that her grandfather had sold him the ranch to protect her from the Broadhowers and the Folsoms, but she knew better.

She had been raised by the man and knew him like she knew herself. Colt Travers was not here to protect her from this or that groom… He was here to be the groom.

Granddaddy was a thorough man. He would want her to be protected by a husband, not a neighbor. That's why he had left her the carousel, so that she would be surrounded by Mr. Travers…nowhere to run…nowhere to hide.

In the moonlight, Holly Jane watched the wind rip the leaves off the trees, whip them about in the air then tumble them on across the earth. Her ribs fairly ached with shivering and, she had to admit, rebellion.

She had never been disobedient to her grandfather during his lifetime, but he knew her as well as she knew him and she was taking a stand.

Colt Wesson Travers was the embodiment of the man she told her grandparents that she would marry. As a dreamy adolescent, she had described him in vivid detail on a daily basis. Granddaddy would have recognized him as easily as she had.

Had she ever guessed that a man existed who fit her fantasy description to a letter, and that Granddaddy would find him and sell him her land, she would have kept her mouth shut.

Oh, but the wind had a bite. She yanked the tarp over her head and squeezed her eyes tight. No matter what happened she was not going to go into that house.

Granddaddy was not going to reach out from beyond the sky and force her to wed.

If she could dodge the Folsoms and duck the Broadhowers, she could elude her neighbor, as well.

And what Granddaddy had failed to take into account was that Colt Travers did not appear to be the marrying kind. He was bad-mannered, bold, certainly not a gallant man like the one of her dreams. He was clearly used to having his way and—

All of a sudden her behind lifted off the carousel and Colt carried her, wrapped up in the tarp. She twisted, trying to wriggle out of the arms that banded her, but they only held on tighter, pressing her against his very solid chest.

It would be a lie to say that this chest was not an

exact fulfillment of her dream lover's chest, but she pushed away from it anyway.

A deep, rumbling laugh vibrated her fingertips. "Time to come home, Snowflake."

Chapter Four

Buried in the tarp, all Holly Jane saw was a dark blur of rough canvas, but she knew the instant Colt Travers hauled her across the threshold and into the parlor. Heat from the large fireplace replaced frigid, howling wind. Flames snapped and fizzled in the hearth. With all her strength, she kicked her feet and flailed her arms, trying to escape the folds tucked all about her.

"Let me go!" She jabbed her elbow into his ribs, but she might as well have slammed it into a log wall.

The infernal man laughed, blame him. His deep rumble tickled her body where it pressed against his chest.

She felt the jerky rise and fall of her weight as he mounted the stairs...two at a time, it felt like.

She heard his boot kick a door then the door slam

against the wall. She winced, but it was his house, after all.

She felt herself falling. Her backside hit the mattress of her bed.

"You, Colt Travers, are a brute," she sputtered, digging her way out of the tarp.

"It's the Travers way." He cocked his head and smiled down at her. Not only did he appear to find her situation amusing, he clearly enjoyed the physical power he had over her.

"You can't keep me here… It's kidnapping."

"That's the Travers way, too."

She freed herself from the tarp then leaped off the bed.

"Stand aside, I'm going home." When he didn't, she made to go around him, but he stepped left and blocked her way.

"You are home."

It felt like home…smelled like it, too, but— "Not anymore. I'm not."

"I'm inviting you politely to stay." He filled the doorway with his big, invasive body then leaned against the jamb.

"I'm declining." She stepped close to him and hoped he noticed the spit and determination in her glare. She would not spend a night in a house that felt like home but with other people living in it. "Kindly move out of my way."

He shook his head. Collar-length hair, brown and

sun streaked, dipped across his forehead. It brushed his cheek, obscuring one of his dimples.

"I reckon your grandfather would have a thing or two to tell me on judgment day if I let you freeze to death."

"I'm leaving." She lifted her chin, clamped her jaw tight and prayed that she looked firm…resolute. "If you try and stop me, I'll scream."

"Have it your way."

All of a sudden he lunged at her, scooped her up and dumped her back on the bed. Before she could let out a screech, he'd climbed in beside her and wrapped her tight in his embrace.

"If you scream, you'll scandalize Grannie Rose and Aunt Tillie." He arched his brows. His eyes conveyed a searing blue challenge.

He was a devil, and no doubt about it. His thigh crossed her hip. He hugged her bosom close to his chest with his big open hand pressing the small of her back. Heat and temptation curled about her in a sinuous wave, brushing her hair, her belly and twining down her legs.

"I'll bake you a cake if you get out of my bed." She offered her proven weapon, but he shook his head.

"Got all the sweets I want right here." He touched a lock of her hair and gently pulled it. It twisted about his finger, gleaming in the soft lamplight. She'd yank it free but she was stuck.

"I've got a deal for you to think about," he murmured, and let her hair go slack on his finger. "You promise to sleep in the house and I'll get out of your bed."

She could refuse... But did that mean he'd stay here all night making her feel... Never mind that.

He was the devil, all right, and charming enough to whisk the bloomers right off her if she weren't careful.

"If it means that much to you, I'll stay." She made sure her voice sounded good and grudging.

He eased out of the bed and took the warmth with him.

"But only this one night," she clarified.

"Guess that means I'll meet you here in bed tomorrow night and every other one you try and spend outside."

"You ought to be locked up. You're just a crime short of being a criminal."

For whatever reason, her insult made him laugh and mention the Travers way again. He kept on laughing, too. She listened to the disturbing timbre of his voice while he walked down the hall then descended the stairs.

A gust of wind hit the window, shook it like a fist. She snuggled into her pillow grateful to be in her bed with her blankets over her. What made her think that she could survive outside with the cold weather coming on?

Pride in all its foolishness, she reckoned. Still,

she wasn't ready to let go of it entirely. Self-respect counted for something.

That meant in order to save face she'd have to act out some sort of objection to remaining in the house. She only hoped the price was not beginning each night in bed with Colt Travers.

"How great a folly is it to lie to one's own self?" she asked the wise old owl who circled the night sky beyond the window.

A couple of things had kept Colt from getting more than a few moments of sleep last night.

He walked across the yard in the predawn listening to the crunch of his boots cut the crisp, quiet morning. He thought about those two things.

One of them was the barn, big and red in the distance setting on top of the rise of a gentle green slope. It had been a long time since animals had lived in it. William had sold off the stock when he became ill.

Colt had been sorry as hell to learn of his friend's passing. But because of William's eagerness for him to have the place, he didn't feel guilty for taking it over.

They had discussed his plans for the horses on those quiet nights they had shared by the fire. If folks could reach down from eternity, he figured William was walking beside him, as excited as he was for the revival of the ranch.

Too bad he couldn't tell him that a dozen horses,

the parents of many to come, were waiting for him at a ranch only a day's ride away. He would bring them home in plenty of time to settle in before the first snowfall of the year.

He only had a week to get the barn ready for them. It would be a challenge, but one he had never really hoped to have. If it hadn't been for William, he would still be sweating for the railroad with only the next payday to look forward to.

A side door of the barn opened then closed. The second reason he hadn't slept last night was now stepping out into the dim light of dawn.

Holly Jane lifted her face to the morning breeze. Her chest rose and fell with the deep breath she took.

Because of her, he hadn't wanted to doze. Each time he closed his eyes he dreamed of her plush little body wriggling in his arms and the sweet brown gaze of a virgin blinking at him with her first stirring of sexual interest. He'd been around women often enough to know when this was the case.

The trouble was, his interest had stirred right back. He'd bet the farm that William hadn't intended him to seduce his granddaughter.

Apparently, Holly Jane hadn't noticed him walking toward the barn. She reached down and patted Lulu on the head, then turned and took the path that led to the bridge, then the lane that went to Friendship Springs.

It took some effort not to laugh and alert her of his presence, but hell and damn, the pig wore a bow of the same blue dotted fabric as Holly Jane's dress. The bow bounced in the piggy ear in time with the sway of Holly Jane's skirt.

Since Holly Jane didn't see him watching, he looked his fill. She wore her hair loose this morning; it shivered over her back, catching the first rays of sunshine.

A raccoon rustled out of the bushes and waddled up to her. She patted its head. Then the pig touched noses with the critter.

"What the hell, Bo Peep?" he murmured. He'd never seen anything like that.

He shook his head. Maybe when the time came, he wouldn't have to go through the sweat of rounding up his herd, he'd just ask Holly Jane to give them a whistle.

He swung the big barn door open wide then stepped inside. Sparkling dust motes chased each other in the dawn light that began to peek through the wood slats.

Five stalls lined one wall, and he would add two more to the wall opposite. He meant to have his mares deliver in the safety of the barn rather than on the open land.

A flock of fat hens pecked at seed in a dim corner. Holly Jane must have fed them before she went to work at The Sweet Treat.

Smack in the center of the flock was Sunday dinner. He could nearly taste the crunch of a fried wing right now.

With more work to be done than time to do it, Colt set himself to the task of making the barn his own.

In no time, it seemed, Aunt Tillie came by to bring him the noon meal.

He sat beside her on a bale of hay and gobbled down a hunk of bread with blueberry jam spread all over it.

"How's Grannie Rose this morning?" he mumbled around the bite of crust.

"Mind your manners, boy." Aunt Tillie slapped his wrist.

He grinned at her and winked. He didn't ordinarily eat with his mouth full of food, but his aunt needed someone to fuss over.

"Considering she saw an alligator in the flower garden this morning, she's doing well."

"Is she getting worse, do you think?" It hurt, watching his grandmother's mind falter.

"Sometimes, maybe. Other times she's as sharp as the both of us combined. She still understands when I tell her that the unreasonable things she sees are in her mind…and the main thing is, Colt, she's happy."

"What about you? Will you be happy here?"

She didn't speak for a minute. She sighed then smiled at him.

"Thank you for bringing us here. It's paradise compared to the viper pit you took us out of."

"Too bad Holly Jane had to lose the place for us to get it." He did feel bad about that.

"Your grandmother heard you last night when she got out of bed to use the chamber pot," Aunt Tillie arched a brow at him. "Once you marry the child, she'll feel at home again."

"I ain't getting roped and tied," he said between bites of an apple. "Especially to Little Bo Peep."

"Bo Peep, is it? You seem defensive, Colt. You always call people names when you want some distance... Rose said you kidnapped her according to the Travers way... You said those very words."

"It was late, and she wasn't kidnapped. I just brought her in from the cold so her granddaddy won't haunt me."

His aunt laughed. She stood, kissed the top of his dusty hair and walked out of the barn.

He wasn't comfortable with the way she kept on laughing all the way out into the warm afternoon.

He set to work, rucking out stalls and repairing broken boards. Working up a good sweat ought to get his mind off matchmaking old ladies and back where it belonged, ankle-deep in straw and dried-out manure.

It had been six days since the Travers family had taken over Holly Jane's home and, she had to admit, the world had not ended. In some ways life had improved.

For instance, because Colt had spread the word

that the ranch belonged to him, she was able to sit beside the spring in Town Square without a single suitor pressing his suit.

She closed her eyes and felt the bliss of fall sunshine kneading her shoulders. She listened to the spring's bubbling water and a bird chirping in a tree that shaded the porch of The Sweet Treat.

Not only were things different for her in town, but at the ranch, as well. When she returned this evening, the house wouldn't be cold and empty. A fire would already be laid in the hearth. Grannie Rose would be laughing about the monkey she had seen poking about the garden and wasn't it a shame that she was the only one who could see the amusing little creature.

Aunt Tillie would be preparing dinner, and the welcoming scent would greet her as soon as she stepped onto the bridge.

If only Colt weren't there to tease her with a grin that meant more than a friendly "How do you do?" With any luck, he'd be working late in the barn getting ready for the horses he was bringing to the ranch.

If not for his disturbing presence, life would be pleasant, easy as a cloud passing though the sky on a summer day.

Because of his high-handed behavior, she had been forced to put on a grand show of defiance, of independence. In the end, though, when it came to a choice between a cold sleepless night outdoors and her warm bed... Well, pride be hanged.

She'd played the game with Colt the first night and the second, with her shivering at the carousel and he toting her back inside.

It hadn't taken long to discover that Colt Wesson was not a man to toy with. He possessed weapons that made her want to fall into his arms...to wrap herself around him and do...something... And it was far from proper.

She could only hope that when she went home this evening he wasn't sitting in Granddaddy's fireside chair polishing a saddle or reading the *Friendship Springs Gazette*. What she would enjoy most was chatting with the old ladies until bedtime without having to constantly be glancing in Colt's direction to see if he was glancing in hers.

Oh, phooey! Holly Jane set all thoughts of the blasted man from her mind and snuggled deeper into her peaceful moment of sunshine and soothing sounds. Really and truly, she felt content for the first time since Granddaddy's passing.

She still intended to buy back the ranch, but for today she was happy to sit in the sunshine and feel good.

A gunshot rang out from the north end of town, shattering her reverie. All around her, shutters banged closed, and folks ran for the nearest open door.

It could only be the Broadhowers and the Folsoms at each other again. The only thing to do was hide from the stray bullets being fired. It would be good to have a town marshal who would not cower under his desk. But that was not the case. She supposed they were lucky to have a lawman at all. Because of the Folsoms and the Broadhowers, no one wanted the job.

She snatched up Lulu and turned in time to see Colt running down the boardwalk. Midstride he snatched up a pair of little boys who had been playing marbles. With one child under each arm, he ducked inside The Sweet Treat.

She dashed in behind him, closed and locked the door.

"Get under the table, boys," she said, then grabbed a plate of cookies from the counter and slid it under with them.

Lulu scrambled in after the children.

Colt grabbed Holly Jane by the waist with both hands. He shoved her against the wall that separated the outer room from the kitchen then pressed her against it with his body tight enough that she could count his slow, steady heartbeats. That had to mean he could feel her quick and erratic ones.

With any luck he would think she was trembling for fear of the men terrorizing the street. He wouldn't know that she was used to them disrupting the peace.

What she wasn't used to was being breath to breath with a man…this man in particular. The scent of his skin, so warm and manly where his pulse throbbed in his neck, is what made her heart loop-de-loop.

A pair of angry voices cut the air only a block away.

She felt Colt's muscles flex and stretch against her bosom and heard the whisper of steel against leather as he drew the long knife from its shield.

"Get under the table with the boys," he whispered in her ear. "Don't come out until I get back."

"You can't go out there!" She reached for the front of his shirt and snagged a button, but it slipped through her fingers.

He opened the door a crack then nodded his head toward the table, ordering her to get under it.

Since Colt, the newcomer to Friendship Springs, was the only one to have the courage to stand up to the town bad boys, she would cooperate.

She got down on hands and knees, lifted the tablecloth and crawled in beside the boys.

"We always like taking shelter with you, Miss Munroe," one of the boys said through a mouthful of cookie crumbs.

"Don't that stranger know to wait ten minutes after the last shot to go outside?" said the other.

"He's new in town. I reckon nobody told him that."

A yip of pain from beyond the door had the boys looking at each other, eyebrows raised in surprise. Heavy-footed boot steps stomped down the boardwalk.

Two minutes later the door opened and Colt peeked inside.

"You boys go along home now."

"But it hasn't been ten minutes." They looked at the plate of cookies then at Holly Jane.

"Fill up your pockets and run along."

Colt stepped inside as the boys passed by him, both his hands hidden behind his back.

"You got an old rag, Sunshine?"

Holly Jane got one from the kitchen then gave it to him. He wiped a smear of blood from the blade.

She gasped and he shrugged.

"Wasn't as bad as it looks." He put the knife in its sheath and shoved the bloody cloth in his pocket. "Just gave the fool a knick on the wrist to make him drop his gun."

"Folsom or Broadhower?"

"Don't rightly know. The one who was pointing his gun at me. Doesn't matter, really."

"It might— The Broadhowers are meaner than the Folsoms." Holly Jane let out a sigh and then brushed a streak of hair away from her mouth. "You might have been killed."

He laughed. "Nice to know you care, but those fools were clowns. It was clear as air that neither of them know one end of a six-shooter from the other."

"That may be, but they might get lucky... And now you've made enemies of them both."

"Pick me out a cake for Grannie Rose and I'll walk you home."

"I can't close up yet. It's only three o'clock and I've still got sales to make."

"I'll take that pie and all the cookies in the case and we'll be on our way." He reached in the pocket of his shirt, then handed her ten dollars.

"That puts me closer to buying you out, thank you very much."

"Not sellin', Sunshine. Not for a million dollars."

Chapter Five

The walk from town was short, the path gentle and flat with big trees to keep the sun off and rustling leaves to listen to.

Even so, Colt figured Holly Jane would be safer if she rode a horse. When he picked up his herd, he'd give her one that was gentle but smart and fast.

Just because the Folsoms and the Broadhowers were leaving her alone for the time being, didn't mean that they would forever. It might not take long before they figured out that, while marrying Holly Jane would do no good, kidnapping her might. Ransom could be a powerful tool. He'd learned that and more growing up.

Could be that Grannie and Aunt Tillie weren't safe, either. He'd give up his ranch for any one of them if it came to the worst, but there were some Folsoms and Broadhowers who might not live to enjoy it.

"What makes those two families hate each other

so much, anyway?" he asked, while they walked beneath leaves that flashed their fall colors in the breeze.

He walked slowly, enjoying the warm afternoon and watching light and shadow flit across Holly Jane's fair-skinned face.

Lucky thing his hands were full of cake and cookies since there was something about being alone with her that made him feel like wrapping her up in his arms and kissing her.

Odd, she wasn't the kind of woman who normally stirred his blood. Too innocent and dewy. What would she see when she looked at him? A criminal, no doubt, like the rest of his kin.

In spite of what Grannie and Aunt Tillie believed, Holly Jane was not the one for him. He needed someone sultry, provocative…a woman of experience, who would pass in and out of his life with no more trouble than a whiff of smoke.

"They didn't always hate each other." Holly Jane plucked a flower from a bush growing beside the path, sniffed it then slid it behind her ear. "A long time ago when my grandfather, old man Folsom and old man Broadhower were young men, they were fast friends who came from the east and wanted to settle near each other."

"Something went the hell wrong."

"And in a hurry. They found the land with the spring, and they bought it. They named their little settlement Friendship Springs. Each of them had ranches that adjoined the other. Granddaddy had the most money so he got the best parcel. The one with the river. It didn't seem a problem because Broadhower and Folsom both knew Granddaddy would never try to dry out their land."

"Sounds peachy so far."

"Fine and dandy until the wives came along. The Broadhower bride and the Folsom bride hated each other. My grandmother said they were both vain and disagreeable women. After being away for a year, Mr. Broadhower came home to find his wife nursing a newborn. She told him she had been raped by Folsom. Mrs. Folsom exposed her as a harlot and a liar, then because of it she ended up beaten and left with a scar on her face. When Mrs. Broadhower fell and broke her leg, then died of the infection, it was all the Folsoms' fault. It might have been, for all anyone knows. They were all crazy with hatred by then."

"Looks like they never heard of forgive and forget."

"There was a time…" Holly Jane smiled, but it was a sad and wistful. The tender expression on her face made his heart squeeze.

"What time was that?"

"So long ago that the families don't remember it." Sunshine, hanging low in the sky glinted off her eyes. Old memories seemed to be making her tearful. "It had to do with my carousel."

"You don't normally see one smack-dab in the middle of a ranch."

"Granddaddy bought it for me."

"Didn't know he was such a rich man."

"Oh, it didn't cost him anything. There used to be a traveling circus that came to Friendship Springs every summer. They rented land from Granddaddy. They'd pitch a tent and set up the carousel. One year they didn't have the money to pay so Granddaddy took the carousel instead."

"I reckon you were the envy of the town."

Her childhood would have been as unlike his in every way there could be.

"Every Sunday after church Granddaddy invited the children from all around to come and ride it. The Folsoms and the Broadhowers got along just fine without their parents to poison their fun."

"Maybe we ought to fire that carousel up again."

"Too bad the old steam engine quit. It could be like old times. The Folsoms and the Broadhowers riding and laughing…having peaceful fun. We could have ourselves a big party for the town."

He'd be able to repair the engine without breaking a sweat. A nostalgic party might not be enough to reunite the families, but who knew? Maybe they could invite the town preacher to keep everyone behaving decently.

They walked in silence for a time. He wondered if she was thinking about how much money it would take to buy him out.

"Colt…" She touched his sleeve as soon as they stepped onto the bridge.

He stopped and turned, gazing down at the loveliest face he had ever seen. He thought for half a second that he might want to look into her eyes forever. It took a good mental shake to remember the only kind of women who had ever wanted him.

"I owe you an apology," she said.

"You load up the cake with salt instead of sugar?"

A frown shot across her fair forehead. A breeze lifted the curls at her hairline. "It's a very good thing that I didn't. I'd have felt wretched over it. I do apologize for messing the house…for not being more welcoming to you and your family."

"I wish I could apologize for pulling your land out from under you, but I can't. A place like this one has been in my blood since I was a kid." He gazed far out, looking it over from tree line to tree line, from green pastures to the barn. His heart swelled. "I'm sorry you lost it, but I'm damn sure grateful that I got it."

"Granddaddy had a reason for selling to you."

"I knew that. Trust me—you'll never marry anyone against your will. I promised your grandfather… and I promise you."

She sighed then very boldly reached up and touched the beard stubble on his cheek. He felt like he'd been hit by a lightning bolt and dumped on by a gallon of honey all at once.

"I knew Granddaddy as well as I know myself. I know how he thought and the reasons for everything he did." She withdrew her hand and arched a fine brown brow at him… She grinned suddenly. "It's true that he didn't want me to marry a Folsom or a Broadhower…he wanted me to marry you."

She turned and skipped across the bridge with the damn pig trotting behind like a bouncing pink ball.

Never in his livelong life had he ever been taken so off guard, so hit from behind…so cut off at the knees.

"It's chilly this morning," Grannie Rose declared, kneeling in front of a pumpkin vine in the garden. "That must be what's keeping the alligator away."

Holly Jane knelt beside Grannie Rose and watched as she cut a fat orange squash from the stem. The old woman's hand was as steady as her own.

"Remember, Rose," Aunt Tillie said from where she stood beside a cornstalk, plucking an ear. "The alligator only exists in your imagination. He isn't real."

"That's a comfort." Grannie Rose sighed. "It will be safer for the monkey now."

"Rose, dear—" Aunt Tillie dropped an ear of corn in the canvas bag tied about her waist "—there is no monkey, either."

"Are you sure? He seems so real."

"I'm sure. Holly Jane will tell you that's the case."

"I haven't seen a monkey since the circus used to come here when I was a little girl."

"A circus in your own backyard! What a marvel. Colt Wesson would have loved that when he was a boy.... That is him over yonder mending the corral fence? He's not a vision?"

Blessed morning, he was a vision all right, carrying posts and swinging a hammer, working up a sweat without his shirt on even in the cold air. She shouldn't look at him, but how could she help it? Name a woman who could.

All right, Aunt Tillie, then. Aunt Tillie was not looking at him; she was looking at Holly Jane and quite intently.

"You know, Holly Jane, Colt comes across rather rough, but he's a very good man."

"Not your typical Travers," Grannie put in. "It always caused him trouble growing up, being such a good boy."

"Why would being a good boy cause him trouble?" That was curious.

"It's not the Travers way," Grannie answered. "Poor little mite. His pappy, my son, had his heart set on Colt being a gunfighter. Used to boast about it when Colt was just a baby."

That explained his name, then.

"You can imagine the trouble it caused when Colt refused to even pick up a gun." Aunt Tillie glanced at her great-nephew, pride apparent in her smile. "Being a good boy did not mean that Colt was not a rebel. If his pappy said turn left, Colt turned right. If he said sit down, Colt stood up."

"One day when he was twelve years old—isn't that right, Tillie, twelve?—his pappy told him to take the hundred dollars they had just robbed from a family, home to the hideout while the rest of them went to another town to rob the collection plate at a church. Our boy didn't take to thievery, so he hid out in a gully with the money. Then when it got dark, he went back to the house that was robbed and dropped the money on the front porch."

"He carried the bruises for that an entire month." Tillie frowned and dropped a cob into the bag.

"And proudly." Grannie Rose nodded, her gray hair sparkling silver in the sunshine. "That's about the time when all the other boys were learning to shoot. Naturally, Colt would have none of that and took up knife-throwing instead. His pappy nearly had a fit and would have gone after him with a whip, but Tillie said she'd use it on him if he tried. Everyone always listened to you, didn't they, sister?"

"Not when I told them crime was a mortal sin. They laughed at that."

"What was the worst thing Colt ever did?" Fascinated, she couldn't keep herself from asking. His past was as different from hers as day was from night. Since he was born and raised a criminal, she couldn't help but wonder who he really was now. Devil, angel or someone in between?

When she thought about it, what was to keep Colt from drying out both the Broadhowers and the Folsoms and taking their land?

"He used to set hostages free." The pride in Aunt Tillie's voice was unmistakable.

"The whole family carried on about how he prevented them from collecting the ransoms. Didn't make no never mind to Colt Wesson, though. I don't think we ever did collect a ransom, did we, Tillie?"

"Nearly, once, when Colt was sick with a fever. But he recovered in time to take the money and the young captive home."

"What happened to him? Was he punished?"

"He has a scar, but Pappy came away from that beating with two. That's the day when Colt Wesson figured he was too big for beatings and lit out on his own." Grannie cut a small pumpkin then set it beside the big one. "My son was a good Travers, but not a very good man."

From across the field she saw Colt finish his repair of the corral gate. He swung it open and closed three times, testing it. Then he put his shirt back on and went inside the barn.

Just because she felt gooey inside when she looked at the man, just because she felt weak in the knees when he looked at her, did not mean that she was in love.

Love did not happen in a blink. It took time to bloom then grow. It was founded on mutual respect… upon putting the other person's best interest over your own.

It was a slow, steady progression of friendship into an unbreakable bond.

That odd feeling she had whenever he was near,

the one that made her want to snuggle close to him could not possibly be love.

But she could be wrong.

All of a sudden, squawking erupted from the barn.

"Looks like chicken and dumplings for dinner, sister."

It had been too many years since Colt had tasted Aunt Tillie's chicken and dumplings.

He held the black hen upside down by the legs. She was plump, pretty and delicious looking. There would be a feast tonight.

She was a squawker, though. Her caterwauling had to be reaching town. Damned if his eardrums weren't about to pop.

He'd best wring her neck quick and get it over with.

With his thumb and fingers looping the soft feathers, he suddenly felt his balance shift.

One moment he had been dreaming of dumplings then the next he found himself lying on a pile of hay with Holly Jane on top of him pounding his chest with small closed fists.

The chicken wasn't the only one screeching.

"Let her go!" Holly Jane thrashed and wriggled against him, reaching for the bird that he still gripped by the legs.

He opened his hand. The hen strutted away in an

indignant fluff of feathers while Holly Jane scrambled off him.

She stood over him, glaring down fire and brimstone.

"Matilda is a new mother!" Her bosom heaved with her anger.

He smiled, couldn't help it. For all that she was small, Holly Jane was beautifully formed. Better than that, she was a spitfire of a woman. All sugar and spice…lots of spice. Any man would need to keep a good firm hold on his heart when it came to her. She'd have him roped and tied without him even being aware of it.

Once again, he'd best pay attention and remember the women he was suited for. Harlots and loose women would accept him for what he was and not shed a tear when they parted company.

"Those chickens are egg layers!" She kicked a puff of dust and straw at him.

He sat up and brushed a piece of dried-out manure from his sleeve. Looked like he still had some cleaning to do before Wednesday.

"What do you suggest we eat, Bo Peep?"

"Go ask the butcher in town." With that she spun about and disappeared into the henhouse.

A few seconds later she marched out, cupping something between her palms. He'd stood up by then so he peered down to see what it was.

"You were seconds away from making little Joey an orphan." She closed her fingers back up, hiding the black ball of chirruping fuzz from his view. "You, Colt Travers, are a brute."

He watched her march into the henhouse, back straight and pretty round hips swaying.

Lord, help him. He tried to summon a vision of the tawdriest woman he had ever been with and couldn't see her.

Holly Jane sat upon the elephant's back on the carousel watching lamps being lit in the house. Happy yellow light filled one window after another.

She ought to go inside before Colt came and dragged her to dinner. One humiliation for the day had been quite enough.

Even now, hours later, she felt the blush reach her hairline. It hadn't been necessary to push Colt down. Her reaction had been pure temper. She might have calmly explained that these particular chickens were not for eating and that she would gladly bring one from the butcher's shop next time he wanted chicken and dumplings.

"Blame it," she mumbled, turning on the elephant to watch the sun go down behind a bank of clouds. Normally, watching the sunset soothed her, but not tonight.

Even though he had been the one about to murder Matilda, she was the one about to do the apologizing.

She turned back to face the house and found Colt watching her through the parlor window.

An apology wouldn't alter her opinion of him. He was a criminal…a brute. Yes indeed, let her linger here in the dark five more minutes and he'd come marching out of the house to haul her to the dinner table.

High-handed is what he was, bossy and arrogant… and opening the front door.

"You coming in, moonbeam?" he called.

Condescending, she couldn't forget that character flaw. Anyone who called other folks names must have a pretty high regard of himself.

She'd just as well apologize for her aggressive behavior and get it out of the way. Slipping down from the elephant's back, she walked toward the house. Colt came down the steps and met her halfway.

"Sorry about your hen," he said "Didn't know she was a pet."

That was mannerly of him; she would have to give him his due. Then again, what kind of apology was it when it was delivered with a grin and a flash of dimples?

"It was an understandable mistake." And it was, really, now that he was sorry for it. "Most fowl are livestock."

They walked in silence for a moment, watching an owl circle the darkening sky and clouds gliding in like a blanket.

"I'm sorry I knocked you down."

"You pack a punch, for a little bitty thing." Even

in the dim light she noticed the glint of humor in his eyes. "You did catch me by surprise, though."

"You gave me cause."

"What do you say we call it a draw and go in to dinner?" He winked at her. "It's pork chops."

He quickstepped it to the porch.

"You are not a funny man, Colt Travers!"

She dashed past him and up the stairs so he wouldn't see her grudging smile.

Aunt Tillie and Grannie Rose set four plates on the dining table and one on the floor for Lulu.

Colt pulled out chairs for all three of them. Grannie Rose patted his cheek; Aunt Tillie smiled. Holly Jane sat down, avoiding eye contact with him.

They joined hands for the blessing. Holly Jane held one of Grannie Rose's hands and one of Aunt Tillie's. They bowed their heads while Aunt Tillie gave thanks for the cool autumn day and the fact that they did not accidentally eat Matilda.

Supper with the Travers family was a bright spot in her day. Had it been such a short time since she and Lulu had spent their evenings alone? Until now, she hadn't realized how dreary that had been. With the Traverses here, it felt more like the happy times when her grandparents were alive.

It couldn't last, of course. She was going to buy back the ranch. After that, things couldn't help but change.

She came out of her thoughts just in time to see

Aunt Tillie send Grannie Rose some sort of message with her eyes.

"How grand that the horses will be coming home on Wednesday," Grannie Rose announced. "Will you be gone to fetch them just the one night, Colt?"

"If the weather's good and the horses have a mind to come along peacefully."

"It's only a shame that we're too frail to ride along with you. I recall the time I went on a horse raid with your grandpappy…we were so young, very much in love. It was—" Grannie looked lost in the past for a moment, seeing things that no one else could. "Lovely."

"It wasn't lovely for me," Aunt Tillie said with a huff. "I never got a wink of sleep, thinking you all would get arrested and hanged."

"As it turned out, Holly Jane, Grandpappy and I got so involved with our campfire that we never did get the horses. By morning the owner had taken the whole lot of them and moved on."

"Too bad that wasn't the case every time." Aunt Tillie looked as though she saw the past as well, and it was sour as a pickle. "Well, the reason that we are sorry to be frail old ladies who can't travel is because we could both use a new dress. Isn't that right, sister."

"Right as beans."

"Right as rain," Colt corrected. "You two are up to something, I can smell it. You made it here all the way from the Broken Brand without a complaint. An overnight trip shouldn't tucker you, especially with some new duds at the end of the trail."

Grannie Rose and Aunt Tillie glanced at each other.

Colt was right; they were up to something.

"That did tucker us out," Grannie Rose said. "We were just too proud to say so."

"There's a lovely dress shop right here in Friendship Springs," Holly Jane pointed out.

"I'm sure it's charming," Aunt Tillie replied. "But we have our hearts set on something from where the horses came from."

"Yes, a memento of the beginning of Colt's dream."

"Tell me what you want and I'll pick it up," Colt said.

"That's sweet, dear, but you haven't the fashion sense of a flea." Aunt Tillie set her fork on her plate and wiped her mouth with a cloth napkin. "You might accidentally bring something pink for me and blue for your grannie."

"We would like Holly Jane to go along and pick something out for us…and for her. You could use a new frock, couldn't you, Holly Jane?"

"I'd love to help, truly." The very last thing she was going to do is go someplace overnight with Colt Wesson. "But I have The Sweet Treat to run."

"I'd take it as a favor if you'd let me run it for a couple of days," Aunt Tillie said. "I always yearned for a candy shop of my own, but being shut away at the Broken Brand, well, life just passed on by."

"Never heard you mention that particular dream, Aunt Tillie," Colt said.

He might as well have not spoken for all the attention the ladies paid him.

"Won't you please do us old women a favor, Holly Jane? When you come back, we'll all go to church of a Sunday in our new gowns." Grannie Rose looked as pleased with the prospect as if she and her sister hadn't just thought of it.

"We're roped and tied, Sugar Plum," Colt said. "See you at four, sharp."

Chapter Six

Holly Jane listened to the patter of raindrops on the oilcloth that covered her, head to toe, as she sat beside Colt on the buckboard.

It was still two hours before daylight, and she shivered in the predawn chill.

"Just so we're clear," Colt said to Aunt Tillie and Grannie Rose who stood on the front porch of The Sweet Treat with Lulu. "You'll spend the night at the hotel and I'll pick you up tomorrow afternoon."

"Yes, dear, we're clear." Aunt Tillie lifted a lantern. It cast a golden circle around the pair of them standing in the doorway.

"Don't worry about a thing, Holly Jane," Grannie Rose called to her. "We'll earn scads of money while you're gone."

"If you see a Folsom or a Broadhower, lock the door," Colt warned.

Aunt Tillie rapped her cane on the wood porch. The sound echoed around Town Square, silent this early, except for the drip of rain from the eaves and gurgle of the spring.

"I asked the marshal to keep an eye out," Colt said. "Don't give him too much trouble."

"They'll be better off with Aunt Tillie's cane," Holly Jane mumbled.

"So that's a blue dress for you, Grannie, and pink for Aunt Tillie?" Colt asked with a wink.

"Go on with you now, boy. You know what we want." Grannie Rose winked back.

"I do, and it ain't going to happen."

Not in a million years, Holly Jane mentally agreed. Clearly, the old ladies were matchmaking. Granddaddy didn't have a thing on them.

"Let's bring home the horses, Cupcake."

Colt clicked his tongue and jiggled the reins. The buckboard team plodded around Town Square then pulled the wagon north, out of town.

"You think they'll be all right?" she asked, glancing back at the hushed street. The only noise was the plop of hooves in the mud and a baby's cry coming from one of the homes nearby.

"Wouldn't leave if I didn't think so." The baby's cry quit as suddenly as it had started. No doubt the sweet little thing was warm and cozy at its mother's breast. "They lived most of their lives with outlaws. If it came to trouble, I'd put my money on the old ladies."

"Where are we headed?" she asked. In spite of the damp chill and the fact that she had been hoodwinked into coming along, this was an adventure. She hadn't spent much time away from Friendship Springs.

"Thunderson Ranch. We ought to get there late afternoon if the road doesn't get too muddy. If everything goes well, the herd will be in home pastures by late tomorrow."

That was a lot of time she would spend sitting on the wagon bench beside Colt. There were some things she'd like to know about him.

"Colt, why do you call folks names all the time?"

"More sociable than 'hey you,' I reckon."

"I'm not a cupcake."

"I'll keep that in mind, Sunshine."

She frowned hard at him but he kept his gaze focused on the muddy road. From profile, she watched him smile. Whenever he did that his dimples winked. Curse the man for being so handsome. Curse him double for being the image of the one she had always dreamed of, but curse herself even more for telling Granddaddy so.

A criminal...or a former one, was not a man to build a dream upon.

"I don't know how I let them finagle me into making this trip with you," she grumbled.

Colt laughed; a deep rumble shook his chest.

"Well, they're tricky, those old ladies. I've been finagled all my life."

"We wouldn't suit, you know that," she said, and snuggled deeper into the oilcloth. They might suit… unless he wasn't as wonderful as he seemed. For all she knew, after he dried her neighbors' land, he might move his family to Friendship Springs.

"You aren't my type," he answered.

"Good, then. Now that we have an understanding, we can enjoy the ride. I think I'm half as excited to see those horses as you are."

"These ponies are livestock, not pets."

"I wouldn't call them pets so much as friends. I missed the horses after Granddaddy sold them."

"I reckon it was tough for him after the sickness took its toll… Tough for you, too."

What could she say? It had made her weep inside every day watching him grow weaker.

"He sold everything except the chickens. We needed the money to live on until—" Until he died, and she found that the ranch had been sold and she inherited the money from the sale.

That's when she had bought The Sweet Treat. With everything that she had loved gone, except the carousel and the quarter acre of land it sat upon, she needed something to do, a reason to get up every day.

Since she had always loved sweets, both baking and eating them, having her own shop was the balm she needed.

"I'm sorry about your grandfather, Holly Jane. He was a fine man."

Because he wasn't smiling his disarming smile, and because he'd called her by her name, she didn't shove him away when he crossed one arm over her shoulder and drew her in with a comforting squeeze.

When they reached Homerville, the town south of the ranch where he was to pick up the herd, Colt tried to drop Holly Jane off in the bustling town so that she could get the shopping done.

He soon discovered that there was a stubborn little lady under that sunshine disposition. She refused to be left behind because, as much as she wanted to visit the shops, she was even more eager to see the horses.

There had been no help for it but to go shopping with her. Even though the dresses had been a last-minute thought in Grannie Rose and Aunt Tillie's plan, he knew they would be looking forward to them.

He did manage to fit in a meal of steak and eggs into the bargain, though. A man needed his strength when navigating the foreign world of feminine gewgaws.

In the end, he did have to admit that toting Holly Jane's purchases hadn't been the chore he had feared.

Watching her enthusiasm at pleasing the old ladies touched him. For the space of a fly buzzing past his ear, he wondered what life would be like if Holly Jane were his type of woman…and he were her type of man.

But he wasn't and she wasn't.

There was a rough edge to his soul, put there by years of living on the Broken Brand. Even if he wanted Holly Jane, she would never accept him.

At the Thunderson Ranch, in the here and now, the rancher's daughter was his kind of woman. She leaned over the porch rail of the big white house, watching him while he thanked Mr. Thunderson for the horses.

He felt the daughter's interest, nearly tasted it, while her gaze assessed him. Her eyes said that she knew what she wanted, how to get it and had the figure to make a man do her bidding.

She stepped off the front porch with a provocative sway to her hips. He doubted that many men refused her call.

"This is a fine string of horseflesh, Mr. Travers," the rancher said while his daughter came to stand beside him. "I wish you the best with them."

They shook hands.

"Papa, can I show Mr. Travers the new colt in the barn?"

"Certainly, Madeline," her papa said. He waved goodbye, then went to have a word with Holly Jane, who stood across the paddock with the string of horses waiting to go home.

It was sadly clear that Mr. Thunderson didn't know what his sweet girl was all about.

Madeline snaked her arm through Colt's. He'd

bet his new ponies that her breast hadn't pressed against him by accident.

"It's dark inside the barn. We'll have to be quiet... so as not to scare the mama. You'll be glad you took the time to get acquainted with the plump, pretty thing," she murmured, drawing him toward the barn. "I guarantee you won't be sorry, Mr. Travers."

He glanced at Holly Jane. She had just finished chatting with the rancher and turned her attention back to the horses.

Sunshine glinted off her hair while she stroked the nose of the very mare that he meant to give her. She was smiling while she spoke to it, probably making friends and giving it a name.

Another horse nudged her in the ribs, and she turned to stroke its long nose. Her laugh tinkled across the paddock.

She glanced up at him with eyes as warm looking as polished amber held to the glow of a lamp. She waved, innocently unaware of what awaited him in the barn.

Flushed with pleasure at meeting the horses, she resembled a fresh spring buttercup. A breeze kicked up and caught her yellow skirt, tugging and twisting it about her knees. It caught a lock of hair and blew it across her fair, pleasure-blushed face.

Holly Jane must be partial to the wind because she lifted her face to it. It caught her hair and streamed it out behind her, glinting like a passel of shooting stars.

Suddenly, and he couldn't say why, the woman clinging to him looked like a weed in comparison to Holly Jane.

"Not today, Tumbleweed." He plucked her arm off his shirtsleeve, then stepped away from her. "Got to be on my way."

Smooth as a polished knife blade was the way that Colt would describe the trip home.

The late afternoon was sunny with a crisp, but easy breeze. Birds twittered in the trees and the future of the ranch looked promising.

The horses trailing on a lead behind the wagon were strong beautiful animals, who would be the parents of generations of strong beautiful animals.

With time to think along the slow ride home, he wondered what it was that had made him walk away from the rancher's daughter. She had been beautiful and more than willing.

The answer came to him easily. He didn't want to see the condemnation in Holly Jane's eyes if she guessed what he had done. It surprised him how much he wanted her respect.

He watched her walking beside the mare he had given her. She talked quietly to the horse, stroking her long gray jaw and calling her Molly.

It was hard to recall when another person's regard had meant a dunghill to him.

He was saved from having to consider what that meant when a pack of farm dogs, five fierce looking ones, came tearing across a field, barking and snarling.

Dogs running in a pack could be dangerous.

The horses stomped and snorted. If they panicked they might be injured on their leads. If he let them loose they'd run scared and be hurt that way.

This was one time he wished he carried a gun. A shotgun blast would send the canines home in a hurry.

"Get up on the wagon," he ordered.

"It will be all right." The blamed female looked at him with a serene smile when she ought to be terrified.

Of all the lame, fool things to do, she walked toward the dogs.

She sat down on the meadow grass and opened her arms to them. The woman was a fifty-foot charge away from being mauled.

"Holly Jane!" he cried, leaping off the wagon. On a run he drew his blade.

"Stay back, Colt," she called.

Like hell!

Halfway to her, he did stop. He stared in surprise when the first mutt halted his charge three feet from her and wagged its tail. The other four did the same. One by one they came forward to sniff her hands.

In another second, they were all over her, rolling and yipping in a frenzy of licking tongues. After a moment of speaking quietly and petting various textures and colors of fur, Holly Jane stood up and walked toward the nervous horses. The dogs followed docilely.

She went to Molly first.

"You see," she told the mare. "They're just barnyard friends. Like the ones you lived with at Thunderson Ranch... Just the same."

Dog noses touched horse noses, and just like that, the entire herd calmed down.

"How the hell did you do that, Bo Peep?"

"Well, Jim Bowie, I nearly didn't with you pulling out that dagger."

He went still to his bones.

Jim Bowie? No one had ever turned the naming back on him. Little Miss Sunshine had spunk. He had to admire that.

"You just turned a pack of mad dogs into lap puppies."

"They weren't mad, just a bit overexcited."

"What is it with you and critters, anyway? They follow you around like you're their mother."

"I can't say what it is, but it's always been that way. I talk to them and they like it."

"Hell, I was going to hire a hand to help with the herd. Might not need to now."

Everyone spent a few more minutes touching noses and getting acquainted.

"Go on home now." She shooed her hands at the pack and they lit out, bounding across the field as though obeying Holly Jane was as good as being scratched between the ears.

Molly laid her head across Holly Jane's shoulder. Holly Jane stroked the horse's ear with slender, delicate fingers while the setting sun bathed them both in golden light.

He stared for a moment, knowing that this was an image he would think of for a long time. He'd carry it in his mind like some folks carried photographic pictures.

It was late, well past dark, when Colt finally allowed a stop for the night.

Wind blew across the open land, cold and piercing.

Holly Jane stood up and stretched the aches from her muscles. She looped her skirt over her arm then hopped down from the buckboard without waiting for Colt to assist her. She gave each of the buckboard horses a pat on the neck then did the same to the new ones tied in two lines behind the wagon.

Colt unhitched the team and led them to a stream several feet from the area he had picked for them to camp for the night.

When he came back he took the others, two by two.

While he was busy with that, she removed the bedrolls from the wagon and placed them on the ground. It would be nice to lie down beside a bright, warm fire, but building a campfire in the wind could be dangerous.

Because there were no trees nearby, Colt tethered

the horses in a circle to the wagon. He picked up her bedroll and tossed it back into the buckboard bed.

"You'll freeze sleeping on the ground."

He put his hands on her waist and lifted her onto the wagon.

"What about you?"

"I'll manage."

"Don't be silly, Colt. There's no need for you to spend the night on the ground."

"There sure the hell is." He untied his bedroll and knelt beside it. She noticed his fingers shaking with the chill even though he had gloves on. "I'm not your husband for one thing."

"Don't tell me you never bent a rule, Colt Wesson."

"There are women you break rules with and women you don't. You're the kind to make a fellow stick to the letter of the law. Besides, if I come up there, we've played right in to Grannie and Aunt Tillie's scheme."

"Your lips are turning blue."

"Damn it!" He stood up and chafed his hands together then stuck them under his armpits. He hopped from foot to foot for a moment before he bent down, picked up his bedding and hoisted it into the wagon.

"I like you, Holly Jane. But Grannie Rose and Aunt Tillie are wrong about the two of us."

"Granddaddy missed the mark by a mile...and I like you, too."

"I'm coming up."

Colt clambered over the side. He set up the bedding, one blanket on the bottom and one on the top.

He must intend that they sleep together under the one bed. That is not what she had in mind.

"You look like you're about to sleep with a serpent."

Maybe she was, if his devilish grin was anything to go by…and his last name was Travers.

"It only makes sense to share the body warmth," he explained.

That big muscular body of his would give off a lot of heat.

"We will have all our clothes on, and our jackets," she murmured, thinking out loud.

"Just have to keep our mouths shut about it. Can't let the ladies know."

"Let's get warm." She stooped down then crawled between the covers of the makeshift bed.

He slipped in under the blankets, wrapped his arms about her, and snuggled her up tight.

She knew the second that she felt his heart beat against her arm, the very instant that she smelled the warm male scent of his skin, that she had made a mistake.

There was nothing for it now but to let his heat seep into her. It touched her hip; it swirled about her legs and melted the shivers from her chest.

She couldn't help it… She sighed deeply and snuggled in closer.

"Better?" he asked, his voice rich and husky sounding.

"Much, how about you?"

His head nodded against her hair.

Bitter wind howled over the ground. It rocked the wagon. One horse snorted and another whickered.

"Look at all those stars." She needed something to say since she was a mile from being sleepy. The dome of glittering crystal was the perfect thing to talk about since it put on a spectacular show. It would be a neutral point of conversation, nothing remotely personal about it.

Oh, but he smelled exactly like the man of her dreams. She had to remind herself that Colt Wesson might not be a dream, but an outlaw…a nightmare.

Who was he, really? Grannie Rose and Aunt Tillie thought the world of him, but they would—he was their baby.

"I want you to know how much I thought of your granddaddy," he said, watching the stars but apparently not wanting to join her in talking about them.

"He and Grandma were everything to me. I don't like to think about what my life would have been if it hadn't been for them."

"Your Granddaddy and I used to sit up late when all the other hotel guests went up to bed. I just want you to know that we got to know each other well. He didn't sell the ranch out from under you just to hand it over to a stranger."

"He never told me about you." The news of the ranch being sold had been a complete shock.

"I expect he should have. He told me about you. He never said you were so pretty, though." Colt stated it as a fact, not a compliment.

"We talked about your ma and pa, too. He told me that when he and your grandma got word of your daddy's death, it near killed them both."

"I guess Granddaddy really did take a liking to you. That's not a story he told to everyone."

It meant something that Granddaddy trusted Colt. Maybe it meant she could, as well.

No one but Mama had known that Holly Jane was on the way when her father had been killed in a hotel fire. Daddy had died saving Mama. Seven months later Mama had shown up at the ranch ready to give birth. Grandma and Granddaddy took her in. A year later the circus came and set up on the ranch, like they always did. This time, when the circus left, so did Mama.

"He told me that you gave them their lives back." He pointed up at the heavens. "Did you see that star shoot across the sky?"

"I must have blinked and missed it." Stars were such a mystery. It was lovely to watch them while she felt warm and safe with Colt wrapped all around her. They had never looked so pretty. "Don't you wonder where they go? Do they settle somewhere else and shine again?"

"Could be, or they just keep on going." He was

silent for a moment, watching the show in the sky. "Like folks. Some stay put and others shoot off to somewhere else."

"Like my mama, I reckon. Grannie Rose and Aunt Tillie said you left home."

"Had to. But it turns out I'm not one to keep on going. Because of your granddaddy I get to settle."

"Yes…and I'll watch you from my carousel." She didn't intend to sound resentful, but there it was.

"As long as I own the ranch, you have a home."

She wanted to believe that, but it wasn't something she could count on. She would work hard at The Sweet Treat to insure her own financial future.

He must have turned his attention away from the stars and to her because his voice ruffled the hair on her temple.

"I'm sorry things worked out for you this way. I know it wasn't fair, but your granddaddy meant what was best for you."

He had, she knew it. Had he not sold to Colt, unsuitable suitors would still be after her. How long would it have been before one of them could not be placated with a chocolate cake?

"I'm sleepy now," she said because she didn't want to talk any longer. "Good night, Colt."

"Holly Jane?"

Cold fingers touched her cheek. He turned her face toward his.

He kissed her in a sweet and brief, tender brush of lips.

"Sleep tight."

A moment later she felt his chest rise and fall in the slow regular pattern of sleep.

Wind rocked the wagon. Horses stomped and whickered. The steam of their breath rose in puffs all about the buckboard.

Up in the sky one star shone brighter than the others. She watched it drift halfway across the sky before she fell asleep to dream of an outlaw capturing her heart.

Chapter Seven

The string of horses tied on the back of the wagon stirred up a heap of dust and a whole lot of attention as they came down the main street of Friendship Springs.

Much of it, Colt noticed, was admiration for the beautiful creatures.

A boy about ten years old followed their progress on the boardwalk, his face eager and full of dreams. Time flashed backward and Colt was that boy.

Had it not been for the twist of destiny that made a locomotive break down, he would never have met William Munroe. He might still be standing on the boardwalk watching other folks' dreams come true.

He wouldn't have met Holly Jane.

He didn't know what made him kiss her last night. Her lips had been full and shining by starlight, her round firm breast pressing close to his heart and her breath puffing warm against his neck… But it wasn't any of those things.

The kiss hadn't sprung from body urges, even though she proved to be curvy in all the right places. It had been an expression of comfort since she had been hurting over the loss of her grandfather and the ranch.

Heartache is what she had inherited. It wasn't right that all she had left was a small piece of ground and a broken-down carousel. There was The Sweet Treat, but that wasn't much considering all she had lost.

Not only had she lost most everything, but she'd gained a guardian that she figured she didn't need.

If he were in her place he'd be spitting mad. Holly Jane was a better person than he was, though. Once she'd made her point in messing the house, she'd treated Grannie and Aunt Tillie like kin.

On the surface, William's actions did seem to wrong Holly Jane, but Colt knew that the man had done the only thing he could. She needed protection.

They hadn't even reached Town Square and already he'd seen two men lounging against a hitching post glaring at the herd.

An elderly man burst out of the barbershop with shaving cream covering half his jaw. He didn't bother hiding his animosity. Colt guessed the fellow was old man Folsom, William's onetime friend.

It wasn't in either family's best interest for Colt's ranch to prosper. If it failed, whichever family strong-armed their way in would cut off the water to the other.

Because Colt was the owner of William's ranch, for the moment, Holly Jane was not a pawn in their game. He aimed to keep it that way. But the time might come when they discovered that she still owned a bit of it…a bit that the water flowed through.

When they reached The Sweet Treat, Grannie and Aunt Tillie waited for them on the front porch. The pig slept in a patch of sunshine with her curly pink tail twitching at a fly.

Colt jumped out of the wagon quick, before Holly Jane could scramble down. More than one woman had caught her skirt on a hook or a bolt and taken a tumble to the ground.

With his arms reaching up for her, there was nothing for her to do but fall into them. She set her hands on his shoulders while his rounded her waist.

It struck him that this is where his hands belonged…on Holly Jane, caressing her curves as though she might consider him her equal.

Hell, it wouldn't be a hardship to let his hands linger a moment, but Grannie and Aunt Tillie watched like birds spotting an afternoon worm.

"Any trouble while we were gone?"

"Not for us," Auntie Tillie answered. "But Mrs. Evelyn Broadhower bloodied the nose of Miss Ellie Folsom. Some business of who was to get the last ham at the butcher."

"We kept Lulu inside most of yesterday afternoon," Grannie added. "One can't be too careful."

"I assume your trip was a success?" Aunt Tillie glanced hopefully between him and Holly Jane.

"It all went according to plan, not a bit of trouble," he was pleased to be able to say.

"And you got the horses, too." Grannie came down the steps and embraced Holly Jane. "We made you three dollars and forty-five cents and met some lovely people doing it."

"Some Broadhower women and some Folsom women...not at the same time naturally," said Aunt Tillie.

"Lock up, ladies. Let's get these ponies home."

"It's a wonderful herd, Colt," Aunt Tillie remarked as he helped her onto the buckboard. "How will you decide which stallion will go with which mare?"

"What do you say, Holly Jane? You up for the job?"

His aunt and his grandmother turned to stare at him, grins crinkling the delicate skin of their faces.

Well, hell. By calling Holly Jane her given name, he'd all but told the old ladies that they had spent the night tangled up in each other.

The ladies might believe that they'd gotten their way, but what they didn't know is how innocent the night had been.

What he would not admit to them is how very deeply he had been touched by Holly Jane. He'd never known that so many strong, and at the same time gentle, qualities could be wrapped up in one sweet little lady.

Nope, it wouldn't be good to admit that to them when he was having the devil of a time admitting it to himself.

Holly Jane was an innocent. He was not. In the long run, they would not suit.

No matter how he wished it otherwise, his past made him unfit for her.

The ladies wanted someplace special to wear their new dresses, and church, they decided, was the place to do it. After that, the hotel for a fancy supper.

Walking down the lane to town with Grannie Rose dressed in her pink, Aunt Tillie in her blue and she in violet, Holly Jane nearly laughed out loud. They must look like a bouquet of giggling flowers with Colt in his black suit as the stem.

"We haven't been to church in too many years to count, have we, sister?" Grannie Rose said.

"Not since Mama and Papa had to tie us to the pew to keep us still."

Holly Jane hadn't been to church in quite some time, either. She'd feared that her presence might cause a disturbance. Since there was only one place of worship in Friendship Springs, both the Folsoms and the Broadhowers attended.

As it turned out, the Travers group did cause a bit of a stir when they came in, even though they sat in the back row. She didn't think it was because folks were relieved to see her back among the flock in her pretty violet gown. More likely it was Colt Wesson they were interested to see.

Single ladies craned their necks to look at him. Married ladies did, too, but more discreetly.

Word that Colt had broken up a fight between the feuding men on his first day in town had spread, making him into something of a hero.

After the service, the Broadhower family and the Folsom family marched out of the sanctuary stiff-necked, with the men on both sides shooting sullen glares at Colt.

Evidently, the preacher's message on neighborliness had not reached their hearts.

The other members of the congregation gave him a warm welcome, shaking his hand and wishing him good luck with the ranch.

The women seemed especially warm in their greetings. They tittered and cooed. They batted their eyes and let their hands rest overlong in his.

They made Holly Jane want to put salt in their sweets. She slapped her hand over her mouth just in time to keep from telling Hilde Brown to pay attention to her own beau and not Holly Jane's.

She was the one not paying attention to the preacher now. And, by the saints, Colt was not her beau.

She walked away from the group, over to a grove of trees whose red leaves twisted in a cool autumn breeze. Since she didn't feel like smiling, she gave herself some time away until she would be more pleasant company.

Snuggling into her shawl, she leaned back against a tree trunk to wait for the visiting to be over…and to set things straight in her mind.

Just because Colt had kissed her good-night did not mean that he belonged to her. And she certainly did not belong to him.

At least not until she knew for sure the kind of man who could tease a woman senseless with a wink of seductive dimples.

She glanced over at Hilde, laughing and flirting. Her mama, standing beside her, looked as proud as a peahen.

Just because Holly Jane might be a wee bit jealous did not make Colt her beau.

It was true that she had fallen in love with him the moment she first saw him bending over her bed, but no fewer than six of the girls she had grown up with were doing the same at this very moment. That did not make him their beau, either.

Colt Wesson was simply an irresistible man. But resist him, she would. They had agreed on the rules. He liked her and she liked him. The kiss he had given her was nothing more than a friendly wish good-night… It was neighborly, and he was her neighbor. His property wrapped all around hers like a circle around the moon.

She shouldn't look over at the church steps. Hilde

was a persistent flirt. No doubt she had lassoed herself a second beau by now. Although, she couldn't imagine Colt as second to anyone.

A quick peek wouldn't hurt, and with just one eye.

Grannie Rose and Aunt Tillie had flanked Colt, one on his left and the other on his right. Any woman who approached him now would have to converse with the elderly women first.

That shouldn't please her. The Travers sisters were matchmaking.

She and Colt had agreed that they were not meant to be matched up.

Holly Jane stood behind the counter of The Sweet Treat with her chin propped in her hands. She looked out the window, watching the steady drip of cold rain falling on Town Square.

Since the rain began, there hadn't been a single customer. She'd baked and frosted, nibbled cookies and petted Lulu, and now there was nothing left to do but gaze out at the damp weather and think.

She tried to picture the new horses, the chicks in the barn who were now a week and a half old. She wondered what Aunt Tillie would fix for supper, but only one thought stuck in her mind.

Colt Wesson's bare chest.

Before daylight, she had gone to the barn to feed the chickens, just like she always did. This morning Colt had gotten there before her and was cleaning out the stalls.

He'd taken off his shirt to do it.

Lantern light rippled over the lean, brawny muscles of his back as they stretched and flexed.

Her footsteps rustled through the straw scattered on the dirt floor.

She was having the devil of a time forgetting the smile he had flashed at her, the way his dimples flickered in the lamplight. He always looked like he knew something that no one else did.

A sudden knock at the back door saved her from wondering too long what was behind that grin.

Someone wanting in through the rear was unusual.

Lulu woke up from a nap on her rug and paddled through the kitchen to investigate.

Holly Jane opened the door to sixteen-year-old Bethanne Folsom standing under a black umbrella.

"May I come in, Miss Munroe?"

Holly Jane took the umbrella and set it beside the oven.

"Let me get you some hot chocolate."

Bethanne followed her through the kitchen and into the main room.

"Why don't you sit by the table near the fireplace?"

"I'd like one farther from the window, if that's all right."

Holly Jane nodded. "The hot chocolate won't be a minute. Is there anything else you'd like?"

Bethanne studied the pastry case.

"A slice of white cake…and a favor."

"What is it you need?" she asked.

"I'm expecting a guest. Can I have two slices of cake and two hot chocolates?"

"Treats with a guest on a rainy afternoon? It sounds lovely."

"Miss Munroe?" Bethanne said at the same time that another knock sounded at the back door. "My guest is Susan Broadhower."

"I reckon I'd better let her in before she gets soaked through."

Since Susan was indeed soaked through, the girls moved to the table near the fireplace.

Holly Jane set the hot chocolate on the table then brought the cake.

The girls looked nervous, talking and laughing but glancing out the window every other minute.

Holly Jane closed the curtain. She locked the front door and flipped the Open sign to Closed.

"Thank you, Miss Munroe. If our folks caught us together they'd tan our hides, for sure," Susan said around a sip of her warm drink.

"We don't mean to cause you trouble, but we couldn't meet in the woods like we usually do because of the rain."

Holly Jane remembered how tricky friendship had been for her growing up. She liked having friends, but she couldn't be a friend to a Broad-hower child without becoming the enemy of a Folsom child, and the other way around.

With the exception of carousel days, those poor children kept to themselves.

Holly Jane got herself a cup of coffee and sat down at the table with the girls.

"We only want to be friends," Susan said. "Why should we have to hate each other only because our parents and grandparents do?"

"It doesn't make any sense," Bethanne added. "I believe that most of the stories we hear aren't even true."

"With winter coming, you won't be able to meet in the woods anymore." Holly Jane tapped her finger on the table, thinking. "I'm closed on Sundays. You can meet here. I'll leave the key under a stone beside the back door."

"Oh, Miss Munroe!" Susan got up, came around the table and leaned down to give her a hug. "You are an angel on earth."

Bethanne reached for her hand and squeezed it.

"It doesn't have to be just the two of you, unless you want it that way." Holly Jane savored a sip of her hot chocolate, the front of her gown damp from Susan's hug. "Anyone else who needs a friendly place is welcome, too."

"It's hard to say anything... We don't want to get caught."

"I understand. I'll just leave the two of you to

visit." She stood up, cradling the warm mug in her fingers. Lulu followed her toward the kitchen. "And, Susan, move a little closer to the fire."

Colt sat on the corral fence watching the mare and stallion that Holly Jane had paired up. They seemed to like each other well enough. Silver, the stallion, was midnight-black and the mare was as lustrous a brown as Holly Jane's eyes.

Chances are the mare wouldn't be interested in breeding until the spring, but it was good to let them get acquainted in the meantime.

In the distance he saw Holly Jane carrying a pumpkin. She set it on the carousel then went back to the garden and brought another. After she had collected four of them, she sat down on the platform and set one of the big orange gourds on her lap.

His interest perked when she drew a small knife from her apron and began to saw at the thing.

Leaping down from the fence, he walked toward the carousel.

"Halloween will be here and gone before you get anything done with that knife."

He drew the Arkansas Toothpick from its sheath and sat down beside her.

"I've never carved one of these things before," he admitted. "Mind if I give it a try?"

"I know you're teasing me." She passed the pumpkin to him.

"At the ranch I grew up on we had a pumpkin

once. One of my aunts stole it off of someone's front porch during a holdup. All of us children were amazed by the thing, but we never got another one. Show me what to do."

"First you cut the top off, like I started to." She traced a line with her finger around the stem on the gourd.

"What are you going to do with all these?"

The Toothpick made easy work of the top cut. He pulled the plug free and a glob of orange pulp came with it.

"They'll go in front of The Sweet Treat tomorrow night," she said. "All the merchants in the square set them out. We stay open late on Halloween so the town children can come to look at them."

"I reckon Grannie Rose and Aunt Tillie would like to see that." They had missed so many of the joyous things in life being shut away at the outlaw ranch. He aimed to make up for it. "I'll fetch us some dinner from the hotel and we can all watch the younglings together."

Holly Jane stared at him for a moment, her eyes squinting, as though she were trying to figure him out. Hell, he couldn't even do that most days.

"You have to scrape the seeds out next," she said, apparently coming back to the task at hand.

He glanced about for something to scoop with.

"You have to dig them out with your fingers."

She reached her hand into the pumpkin and withdrew a fistful of strings and seeds.

Following her example he dug in and came out with a pawful of slime.

"Do the Broadhowers and the Folsoms get along that night, for the children's sakes?"

"They never come."

"That's a crime."

"It ought to be." Holly Jane shook the seeds from her hand into a pot.

"Why don't you give those to the pig? Looks like she wants some."

"These are for roasting." She scooped out another handful, then he did the same. "I had a pair of visitors to the shop today."

"Which swains do I need to set straight, Folsoms or Broadhowers?"

Holly Jane laughed and the sweet tinkling sound made his belly flip.

"One was a Folsom and one was a Broadhower—now you get to carve a face, happy or scary, it's up to you—but they were girls looking for a place to meet where their parents wouldn't know."

"Brave little souls. What if I carve half the face scary and half happy?"

"Get to it, Michelangelo."

The blade slipped and he came within a hair of cutting his finger. He hadn't had a nick in ten years or more.

"It might not be safe for you to offer shelter. It'll cause trouble if they're caught in your place."

"It will… But I told the girls they could use it on

Sundays during the winter. Really, Colt, somebody needs to help them."

"I reckon you're right."

"Too bad the carousel isn't working. We could fire it up and have a big party. Just like when I was a child."

"I wonder if Grannie and Aunt Tillie ever rode one?" He couldn't recall them mentioning it.

"Can't you see them now in their colorful new gowns, going round and round? Pass another pumpkin over here, Colt."

He set it between them, and she motioned for him to give her his knife. Other than its creator, no one had ever touched the blade—he hadn't allowed it.

"Be careful…it's wicked sharp."

It wasn't easy watching the metal slice through the firm orange flesh of the pumpkin. Any second he expected to see blood spurting from Holly Jane's finger. Couldn't very well insult her by snatching it back, though.

It would seem like he thought she was incompetent, which he did not think at all.

At last she set the blade down and he relaxed.

Holly Jane tugged and twisted the lid off the big gourd. He reached his hand in at the same time she did.

He felt the backs of her small fingers brush against his. A seed slid between them. For half a second her hand jerked away, but then it came back… it turned.

Her palm cupped the backs of his fingers. He pivoted his hand through slick strings and seeds. Small fingertips slowly tickled his palm.

She stared out at the horses who were nudging noses in the corral.

He watched the late-afternoon sun dip below the tree line.

Pumpkin goop and lumpy seeds squished through his fingers as he slid his calloused palm over her smooth one. He laced his fingers through hers, rubbed his thumb across her knuckles.

Hesitantly, she stroked his wrist, and then she turned the full force of her melted chocolate gaze on him.

Someone might have punched him in the gut, his reaction to the amber sparkle was that intense. No seductress he'd ever seduced had been half as enticing.

"For a beginner," she said, "you're doing very well."

"I was tender as a grass shoot when I left the outlaw ranch. I had to learn things quick."

"Colt, do you ever think Grannie Rose and Aunt Tillie might be right?"

"About us?"

She nodded. The setting sun shot her hair with golden shimmers. It grazed her lips in dewy light.

"Don't think so." He withdrew his hand from the gourd and stroked the line of her cheek with his knuckles. He lifted her chin. An orange string dappled with seeds stuck to her jaw. "I reckon we ought to prove them wrong, once and for all."

Prove it to himself, is what he meant. Nothing would spark between them. Only a sordid woman would understand and accept his past.

"That way they won't look at us like we're already standing in front of the preacher." Damned if her voice wasn't breathless with innocent excitement.

What she said shook him, because in his mind he had only seen as far as the pile of sweet, fresh straw in the barn.

He sure as hell saw the preacher, now... Couldn't get the damned vision out of his head.

Holly Jane would never be a visit to the barn. He ought to run while he could because, at this moment, he couldn't swear an oath that the old ladies were wrong.

There was only one way to prove it, and that one way was a pair of lips, full and pink, glistening only a few inches away.

He dipped his mouth, felt the warmth of her breath and inhaled the scent of pumpkin.

Holly Jane leaned into his kiss and very neatly stole his heart.

What began as something as sweet as a butterfly on a flower suddenly flared, burning him like a wildfire in dry grass.

With strands of pumpkin draped over his knuckles he buried his hands in her hair, clutching sunshine and silk in his fingers.

Somehow she managed to crawl onto his lap.

He couldn't tell how much time had passed before they broke apart, panting and staring at each other in surprise.

"You have pulp all over your shirt," she murmured.

He nodded, catching his breath. "You've got it in your hair."

"We'd better stop by the pump before we go inside or Grannie Rose and Aunt Tillie will think they're right."

"I reckon we'll need to scrub up pretty damn good."

Hell, there wasn't enough lye soap in the world to scrub her out of his heart now.

Chapter Eight

As soon as daylight faded, Holly Jane came outside to light her pumpkins. A cool breeze dusted a shower of red leaves from the trees in the square. She stopped for a moment, closed her eyes and listened. She breathed in the scent of fresh evening air.

She knelt and struck a match, then lighted two candles and set them inside a pair of smiling-faced gourds to the right of the front door. She did the same to the pair on the left. These were Colt's creations and really very nice, even though one had a snarling face and the other, half scowl and half grin.

Aunt Tillie and Grannie Rose clapped their hands as the faces came to life with a flickering orange glow.

Hopefully the wind would not blow hard enough to put the candles out.

"Let me get a blanket from inside to cover our

laps," Holly Jane said. "Then we'll watch for children to come."

"Won't it be lovely when Holly Jane and Colt have some children of their own?" she heard Grannie Rose say as she stepped over the threshold of The Sweet Treat.

"Yes indeed, sister. I was beginning to despair that our boy would ever find the one."

She wanted to point out to them that she had grown up on a ranch. She knew that it took more than a kiss to create a child.

Even a kiss as enthusiastic as the one Colt had given her—and as eagerly as she had returned it—would not give the sweet old ladies what they wanted.

Washing up at the pump yesterday evening, she and Colt had both agreed that while thcy had enjoyed their kiss, it had been the result of something in the air. Something that made them behave in a way they would not ordinarily.

He considered her an obligation to be fulfilled. A promise to be kept to her grandfather.

She would do well to remember that the next time she felt like a moth drawn to his flame. He would singe her heart and not even realize he had done it.

That kiss was going to keep her mind occupied for…well, forever. The hot pressure of his mouth, the scrape of his stubble against her cheek…she was certain that shc had been waiting for it all her life.

She would need to be on her guard from now on.

She might lose the heart for buying the ranch back if she were to fall in love…real love, that is…since she was already in some kind of love, with Colt.

Even now she wasn't sure. He loved this ranch as much as her granddaddy had.

If he had been serious about not selling for a million dollars, she had no hope by raising that much money, regardless of how she felt about it.

Holly Jane took the blanket from a closet in the kitchen and folded it over her arm.

She would hold to her dream of buying it back because she had to. Without it, all she had was The Sweet Treat and a circle of the ranch that she had to walk over Travers land to get to.

Outside, she sat down on the bench in between Aunt Tillie and Grannie Rose. She spread the blanket over their knees.

As much as she enjoyed living with them, she was in the end, a visitor. She needed a place of her own, because in spite of the fact that she had told Colt that the kiss meant nothing, and he'd told her the same, it meant a great deal.

It meant that she should not be living under his roof unless she wanted to risk making the old ladies' dreams come true.

Footsteps crunched on the road and she looked up from her thoughts.

Colt strode past the spring, coming from the hotel carrying a couple of dinner trays. His gait was long and smooth. He brought to mind one of the stallions in the paddock…lean, strong and male to the core.

She was saved from having to gawk at him any longer by a pair of children running up to admire the pumpkins.

Colt went inside The Sweet Treat. He came out a moment later with the tray of chocolates she had planned to serve her visitors.

A line of what appeared to be grease showed faintly under his fingernails. Granddaddy's nails used to look that way even though he'd scrubbed them with a brush.

Colt must have been working on the equipment in the barn. It hadn't been used in a very long time.

He squatted and held out the tray to the children.

"Miss Munroe made them special for you, buttercup." He nodded at the pair of them, with a smile. "You, too, cowboy."

Darn those dimples. The more time she spent at her carousel the better off she would be.

Colt dug a broken bolt from his shirt pocket and handed it to the blacksmith.

"Can you make one like it?" he asked.

"Reckon so." The blacksmith scratched his beard and squinted at it. "What's it from?"

"A carousel."

"Holly Jane's carousel?" He held the pieces of the bolt up to the afternoon light streaming in through the open doors. "A weld might work but I reckon you're better off with a new one."

"When can you have it finished?"

"An hour, maybe less… Say, you trying to get that old thing running again?"

He nodded. "It's a surprise for Holly Jane. I'd appreciate if you kept quiet about it."

"No one will hear it from me. Miss Holly Jane is a special little gal, always has been. I used to take my son to ride the carousel on Sunday afternoons. She did her best to see that the Broadhower children and the Folsom kids had fun together. Even way back then she was a baker." The blacksmith's eyes took on a glassy look while he visited the past. "I recall how she would get all the children sitting on the ground under a tree, then she'd pass out the treats she'd made and get everyone talking and laughing. Yes, sir, she is one special lady."

Damned if he didn't think so, too, and that was before the story of the younglings under the tree. If only he could find some fault in her, something that might make him more acceptable in her eyes.

"I'll be back in an hour."

"It's good to have you here in Friendship Springs, Mr. Travers. That was a pretty string of horses you brought in." The blacksmith tugged his apron over his round belly. He picked up a hammer.

Colt figured the fellow must be good at his job. His biceps looked like rocks.

"Good luck with that carousel."

Colt stepped into the sunshine. Even though it was sunny, the first day of November had begun with a hard frost. The chill lingered in the air.

He turned north, toward The Sweet Treat. He'd promised the ladies he'd bring home a pie.

The south side of Friendship Springs wasn't as pretty as Town Square and the north end of town. The liveryman, the blacksmith and the butcher must not have felt the need for flowerpots beside their front doors.

The Watering Can, Friendship Spring's only saloon, was a half mile south of town. Only a trail through the weeds led from Main Street to the saloon. To reach it by horse or wagon one had to take a road that circumvented town.

The better to keep drunk Folsoms and Broadhowers out of town proper, Holly Jane had explained.

And speak of the devils, here came one now, walking south on the other side of the street.

He strutted along with his red hair standing up at the crown and his hands shoved in his pockets. His elbows bowed out against his portly belly.

"Better watch your back, stranger," he heard the fellow call from behind.

Colt pivoted slowly on his boot heel. Dirt crunched under his steps as he walked across the street.

"You crow something, Cock-a-doodle?"

The man's face flushed from his hairline to his bulbous nose.

"That was my kid brother you sliced up."

"You a Folsom or a Broadhower?"

"Henry Broadhower. I'm the mean son of a bitch who's going to make you pay for what you did to Buck."

"Broadhower, huh?" Colt gripped Broadhower's shoulder in fake camaraderie. "Better bring your brothers along."

While Henry wrestled with the hand on his shoulder, Colt neatly tripped him with a boot hook to the knee. He turned the fall to make sure that the man fell face-first onto the road.

After a moment of flailing about, Broadhower scrambled to his knees. There wasn't much blood, but the fellow looked mad as a swatted hornet.

Colt turned his back, continuing on to The Sweet Treat.

"Don't forget to bring your kin," he called behind him.

It was Sunday afternoon. What Holly Jane wanted to be doing was getting to know her new horse. To be firming the bond that had begun with Molly the very first moment that Colt had presented the mare to her.

Instead, she stood at the stove of The Sweet Treat scrubbing vigorously at a spot that she knew would not come off anyway.

What she was really scrubbing at was a memory...a vision...a picture that the stiffest brush would not be able to scrape from her mind…in case she really wanted it to.

Apparently, Colt Wesson enjoyed a cold swim in the river, and he enjoyed it as bare as an egg.

It was pure accident that she had discovered that fact. Earlier today, she had taken the ladies to lunch in town and to visit with some of the older women who met on Sunday afternoons. With Grannie Rose and Aunt Tillie easily making friends, she had decided to come home and do the same with Molly.

The afternoon had been pleasant so she had decided to walk beside the river. She had not anticipated coming around a curve of the bank to a cove where water circled in a pool and seeing her neighbor floating sunny-side up.

He seemed blissfully at one with the water, the trees and his closed-eye appreciation of them. She should know; she had spent special moments in this spot many times over the years.

Blame it, she didn't want him to know she had seen him. There was nothing to be done but duck behind a bush and wait him out.

While the bush provided cover, there were also spaces in the vegetation…peek holes through which she was most blatantly peeking.

She ought to be whipped. The problem was, when Colt suddenly stood up, water lapped his hips, and hugged the curve of his bottom. Mercy, but she would gladly take that whipping. When he shook the water from his hair and sent droplets flinging about, she knew it would be worth it.

For the life of her, she could not look away from the sparkling liquid sluicing over his naked back. He resembled Poseidon rising from the sea, but a thousand times more appealing in the flesh than on the printed page.

The wind came up all at once. Colt's skin pebbled with the chill as he stepped out of the pool. She squeezed her eyes shut and buried her face in her arms.

She'd had no idea that she had it in her to be so rude. She would need to come up with some sort of chastisement and enforce it upon herself.

Drops of water pattered on her hiding place. She heard one smack a leaf over her head…she felt one hit her scalp.

"Like to join me?" Colt's voice crooned.

She opened her eyes to see ten toes wriggling in the dirt in front of the bush.

She looked up, inch by inch. Flogging is what she needed. A respectful woman would have fled from the scene when she first saw him, not continue to ogle him.

And now she'd been caught.

"I'm sorry," she said, but she must not have been truly sorry because she continued to sit in the shrubbery feeling weak at the sight of his firm, bare thighs. Maybe the reason she didn't flee was because she might faint if she tried.

In the end, he laughed. He snatched his clothes from a tree branch and presented his back.

He dressed, but not before she saw… When he bent over… Well, male animals had them too but not like… Oh glory, how had the day suddenly become so blisteringly hot?

"See you at supper." He turned toward her with his shirt unbuttoned and damp hair hanging in front of a blue-eyed expression that clearly found her apology amusing.

Now here she was hours later, too ashamed to go home but not too ashamed to squelch his virile image from her mind.

A key turned in the lock of the back door.

Susan Broadhower stepped inside. "Oh, I'm sorry Miss Munroe. If I'd guessed you were here I would have knocked."

"I'm so glad you came." She greeted the girl with a hug.

"If you don't mind, I've brought my cousin with me."

"That's lovely. Bring as many as want to come."

Susan glanced behind her. "Come on in Cissy, Miss Munroe says it's all right."

Cissy Broadhower came in and stood behind Susan. Being a head taller, she looked shyly at Holly Jane over her cousin's shoulder.

"Since I'm here, I'll fix you girls a snack." She didn't want to go home. The longer she baked the longer she could postpone facing Colt.

"Bethanne is bringing her sister."

With four girls now wanting to defy the family hatred, the future of Friendship Springs suddenly seemed brighter.

"I think that you girls are brave and wonderful." She would help them in any way she could. "You keep bringing friends and I'll keep baking you treats."

An hour later the shop was filled with the scent of chocolate, cinnamon…and the laughter of young women. They visited until an hour before sunset then got up to go home with hugs and promises to see each other next Sunday afternoon.

"Miss Munroe." Bethanne touched Holly Jane's sleeve before she went out the back door. "There's something we reckoned you ought to know."

"Something to do with your young man," Cissy added.

"I don't have a young man, not anyone special," she lied to herself as much as to them.

"It's to do with Mr. Travers," Susan said with a frown. "We think he's in danger. Our uncle Henry had a run-in with him and now he counts him as an enemy."

"He wants to tie him up and drown him in the river," Cissy Broadhower added. "We pay attention when Uncle Henry starts talking mean."

"And that's only the half of it, Miss Munroe." Bethanne frowned and nodded at her sister.

"I heard the men talking at the woodshed the

other day." She shook her head. "The men in my family don't like your Mr. Travers any more than the Broadhowers do. They think that if he wasn't around that they might get the land. They figure maybe it would go back to you and then they could outright force you…not even try to propose anymore."

"We wish we could help," Susan said, "but we're only girls—no one will pay a wick of attention to what we think."

All four girls nodded at the same time, looking disgusted at the thought.

"The more of you who stand together, the stronger you will be. Just be sure and stay safe."

"Thank you." Cissy hugged her neck. "We'll say a prayer for your beau."

"He's only my neighbor!" she called after them as they vanished into the woods.

She was a ninny and no doubt about it. How many times had she gawked at a naked neighbor? Never, she wouldn't have cared to.

Colt made her feel things far beyond neighborly. Watching him come up sleek and bare from the water had made her want to rip off her own clothes.

When he had mockingly invited her to join him, she had nearly done it.

Grannie and Aunt Tillie had gone up to bed an hour ago. Colt peered out the window into the dark. Heavy clouds pressed close to the earth, threatening rain.

He'd seen Holly Jane come home from The Sweet Treat shortly after dark. She'd passed by the house without pausing for a greeting or her supper and gone straight into the barn. After a while she came out but went only as far as the carousel. And that is where she had stayed the whole livelong evening.

He'd planned on teasing her, making light of what had happened at the pool. He never should have been swimming in the altogether during the daylight. He might have guessed that Holly Jane would come home.

It was his fault that she was feeling so wretched and embarrassed.

"Come on, pig. Let's bring that little gal inside."

Lulu twitched her hooves where she slept beside the fireplace but otherwise ignored him. The little side of ham sure did enjoy her comfort.

Colt put on his long duster and went outside. The air felt damp. Rain would be falling soon. In the distance he spotted Holly Jane dragging something in the dirt, a shovel he thought.

What the hell was she doing?

He'd embarrassed her and he shouldn't have. No doubt, she believed that she owed him an apology, but the opposite was true.

If he'd been a gentleman he would have warned her away when he first heard her footsteps rustling along the riverbank, before she ever walked around the bend of the pool. He couldn't say what made him float about pretending to be asleep. Probably the Travers in him.

He sure the hell knew what made him get up and turn his back, though. Miss Holly Jane had riled him, excited him. She had done it by simply peering at him through the brush.

By nature he wasn't a modest man. The human form, designed by the Creator's hand was nothing to be ashamed of. Still, knowing that Holly Jane was looking at him, judging his body, made his carnal urges roar to life. If their past encounters were anything to go by, her urges weren't taking a nap, either.

He had put on a swagger, acted the part of an arrogant bastard, then hightailed it back to the house like his pants were on fire because, hell and damn, they were.

"What are you doing with the shovel, Holly Jane?" he asked, standing across from her over a trench she was gouging into the earth.

"I'm digging a boundary line to divide my property from yours. I don't think it's a good idea for us to live under the same roof any longer." She dropped a shovel of dirt on the toe of his boot. "You are trespassing."

"I owe you an apology," he said, and watched her eyes widen in surprise.

"I hardly think it's you—"

He stepped closer, cupped her face in his hands and cut off her words with a delving kiss that left the both of them breathless.

Boundary line be damned. It might not be right, but he wanted more and so did she.

With an arm under her knees he scooped her up, carried her to the carousel then set her on the back of the elephant.

"Don't move," he ordered.

Chapter Nine

Sitting upon the big broad back of the elephant, not only did Holly Jane want to run away, she never wanted to face Colt Wesson again.

Her behavior of a moment ago pointed out that she was not as ashamed as she ought to be. A truly repentant person would be shoveling a hole to bury her wicked self in, not kissing the man she had humiliated. An honorable woman would not be holding his naked image in her mind, cherishing and polishing the vision so that she wouldn't—

All at once the elephant jerked. The platform shimmied then moved beneath her. She grabbed the pole to keep from falling off. She felt dizzy, off-kilter…and there was music.

A tune that she hadn't heard in years tinkled over the cloud-smothered land.

The platform picked up speed, turning the long-dormant animals in a circle. Her hair blew out in streaming banners.

Gripping the pole, she leaned back to feel the rush of cool wind across her cheeks and the tickle of it on her scalp.

The past fell away, both the recent and the long-ago. It couldn't be, but wasn't that Granddaddy calling her name? She listened with her heart, feeling that it might burst with joy.

It was a pure and sweet miracle to have the carousel spinning cheerfully after all these years. As hard as she tried to hold on to Granddaddy's voice, she knew that it was Colt calling to her.

She opened her eyes to see him standing beside her knee, grinning.

"What do you think, Holly Jane?"

"I think that I'm going to cry." After what she had done to him this afternoon, he had fixed her carousel.

"You look like you're going to laugh."

"I am." And she did. "Come on, Colt. Pick a steed."

He leaped up behind her in one happy bound. She couldn't see him grinning, but she felt it against her hair.

The carousel was enchantment...it was healing. Troubles were chased off by joy for the few moments one spent flying on the backs of the magical creatures.

She turned her head to watch Colt, his face caught

up in pleasure. Years fell away, and she saw the boy he would have been, the child who defied his family to behave in a decent way.

Knowledge hit her smack in the heart. Colt Wesson was not a criminal. He never had been and would not be.

"Is this your first time?" she asked.

"To repair, yes, to ride, no." He slipped his arm about her waist and pulled her to him. "One of the first things I did when I skedaddled from the ranch was ride a big wood pony."

"What was the second?"

"I got a job in a livery. My boss let me stay there, fed me along with his family in exchange for tending his horses."

"Is that where your dream began?"

He shook his head. "I don't know when I decided I would have a ranch. It's always been inside of me, I reckon."

She watched the dark land spinning before then behind her.

"When did you go to work for the railroad?"

"Two years later." His breath skimmed her ear. "I heard the train whistle one day and figured I wanted to see new places. I was hired to keep the cars clean. After that I learned how to repair the engines. I saved every penny I had, and the job paid well enough to buy me the ranch."

Colt Wesson was not a single thing like his no-good relatives. He worked hard for what he wanted and he got it. Even though it was her ranch that he got, she had to admire him.

"I admire you, Colt." His fingers suddenly clenched her waist.

He was quiet for so long she guessed he hadn't heard her.

"I'm going to have a celebration and invite the children of Friendship Springs, just like I used to." She covered his big hand with hers. It felt natural to stroke his rough-skinned knuckles. They were so very different from her own. "Today I had four girls come into The Sweet Treat. They say there are more who want to come."

"Tell me what to do to help." His breath skimmed her ear, closer this time, warm and moist.

Raindrops pattered on the carousel roof. In the past, rain had leaked through holes in the canopy in several spots. She glanced about but the only water coming down dripped off the carousel eves.

Colt had been busy with more than the horses while she had been away at The Sweet Treat.

"I can't believe you did this!" She would have hugged him, but she was facing the wrong way "I certainly don't deserve it after this afternoon. *Thank you* doesn't begin to express how I feel."

"There's something you need to know about this afternoon, Holly Jane."

"I can't imagine what you must think of me. I'll do anything to make it up to you... I swear it on an oath."

She felt his breath skimming her temple.

"Turn around," he said. "Face me."

It was awkward, with knees and elbows bending and stretching but she managed.

At last she faced him, her knees pressed to his thighs in the cramped space.

"Now, just to even things between us, take off your clothes."

"What!" She would have fallen off the elephant, but he caught her wrist. "I can't do that."

"You did say you'd do anything…and it would make us even."

She had said that. She'd made a vow. To back down now would prove that she was not repentant at all. Not only would she be a voyeur, she would be a liar.

"I want to look at you, Holly Jane."

Colt held his breath when Holly Jane reached for the buttons at her collar. He hadn't expected her to do it.

Her fingers trembled. She bent her head, keeping her eyes on her work.

"Are you scared?" He watched while she slowly slipped the little pearl-like balls free of the fabric. "I won't hurt you."

She shook her head and reached behind to unbutton the waist of her skirt.

"Cold?"

She laughed under her breath. "Hardly that."

He helped pull the skirt from under her when she lifted her hips.

She looked up and speared him with her gaze. She slid her blouse down her arms then held it away from her. She let go and it fluttered away into the night.

"What then?"

"I'm nervous. I've never undressed for a man before."

He'd known that. He wouldn't say so, but it pleased him, knowing no other man had been privy to the treasure beneath her frilly white undergarments.

"Take off the rest."

In anticipation, he studied the shape of her breasts where they strained against the pristine white fabric. He caressed her with his eyes and made sure she knew he was doing it.

She hesitated a moment, then lifted the camisole over her head. She tossed it on the elephant's raised trunk. When she wriggled out of her bloomers he didn't help her. Couldn't, he didn't trust himself.

And there she was, sitting astride the elephant's back, naked and not an arm's reach away.

Music drifted among the raindrops. She lifted her arms and plucked the pins from her hair. They hit the floorboards with a ping. Golden loops of hair tumbled over her chest, hiding her from his view.

To his relief, she gathered the curtain of hair in one hand and flipped it over her shoulder.

Her full breasts jiggled slightly with the carousel's rotation. He clamped his hands into tight fists.

If only he could touch her waist, glide his hands along the curves of her hips where they flared over the elephant's sides. If only he could see the sweet pink flesh beneath her curls where it rode the animal's cold wooden back.

"You are so damned beautiful, Holly Jane. You steal the breath right out of me."

And she did. He could hardly find it while he took his time gazing at her, from the plump curve of her bottom lip to the curl of her pretty pink toes.

"Are you angry because I'm looking at you?"

"No."

"I wasn't angry when you were looking at me, either. I knew you were there the whole time… I wanted you to look… I let you do it."

He took off his duster and set it over her shoulders, making sure to keep the lapels well back. He hadn't gotten his fill of seeing her naked body and he suspected he never would. Holly Jane Munroe had touched him in a way he had not expected.

"So," she said, breathing a deep sigh that lifted her chest, "I reckon we are even now."

He nodded. "We can go back to the house with no hard feelings between us."

"Friends again, like nothing ever happened," she agreed.

"I want to touch you."

Her eyes flushed whiskey-warm.

"Touch me, Colt."

He reached forward, felt the silkiness of the hair at her temple glide through his fingers in long loops and whirls. He leaned forward, kissed her cheek then grazed a light brush across her lips.

He settled back, took the weight of one breast in his palm. With his other hand he stroked the length of her thigh. He flicked his thumb across her nipple then rubbed it in a circle. It rose under his palm, and he heard her husky gasp of pleasure.

"I never knew it would feel like that," she whispered.

"There's more, Holly Jane. Let me show you, let me touch you." He inclined his head, indicating where.

She bit her bottom lip and nodded her head. A gust of wind blew in sideways and dusted her fair-skinned belly with raindrops.

"You mean a great deal to me," he said, reaching his fingers toward her curly mound. "I wouldn't be doing this if you didn't."

Gently, he slid two fingers between the elephant's weathered back and Holly Jane's hot, tender flesh. She didn't shy from his touch so he stroked her.

She closed her eyes and he watched her face while he gave her pleasure.

He kissed away her soft moan of surrender. When, too soon, she slid away from his touch, she had captured him.

Her surrender had been his own. What would he do now? She was the one woman he wanted and the one he could never have.

"Things can't be the way they were before," she whispered... She sighed. He caught a note of regret in the tone. "Things just changed between us."

"Are you sorry, Holly Jane?" If she were, he would take it hard. This pure and lovely woman was sure to see him for who he was...a Travers to the bone.

"I'll never be sorry, Colt." The sidelong rain dotted her face and her hair. "Not for this. But I am sorry that I can't continue to live in the house with you and your family. It wouldn't be proper, not now."

It wouldn't be proper, but he was not proper.

And she was right about things changing.

She was no longer simply an obligation to be fulfilled, the spinster granddaughter of William Munroe to be protected from Folsoms and Broadhowers.

She had become important to him.

"I'll move into the barn," he said.

"If you do that, Grannie Rose and Aunt Tillie will think they are right about us."

At this very moment, he couldn't swear on an oath that the old ladies were not right.

"They can think whatever they want, Holly Jane. You need a better man than me. A gentleman...not a Travers."

He slid off the elephant's back.

"Better get to the house before the rain gets worse."

Reaching up, he eased Holly Jane into his arms, being very careful to keep her covered with his duster.

Sleeping in the barn wouldn't be so bad. It would sure as hell beat watching the old ladies count their great-grandchildren.

The first was to be called Emily, the second, Alexander. After that, he and Holly Jane would be allowed to name the children whatever they wanted to.

Hell, he wondered, did Holly Jane know about Emily and Alexander?

It was late. The wind howling about the barn kept him awake, so by lantern light he brushed down the horses, beginning with Molly.

The big red barn was not uncomfortable. With a potbelly stove to keep him warm and the whicker of horses for company, he didn't mind his new home.

The problem was, keeping his distance from Holly Jane would not be as easy as moving to the barn.

She haunted him. If he were honest with himself, he'd admit that it wasn't the wind keeping him awake; it was the image of the woman on the elephant, her ivory skin flushed with pleasure.

No matter if he worked up a sweat raking manure,

stacking bales of hay or cleaning the henhouse, her image remained in his mind.

That hadn't happened even with women he'd been thoroughly intimate with.

No doubt by the light of day, with the enchantment of the carousel and the rainy evening vanished, Holly Jane would hate him. There would never be an Emily or an Alexander.

It would be for the best if she did dislike him. Keeping his hands off her would be easier that way.

He cared for Holly Jane too much to compromise her...more than he already had, at any rate.

A little time and a little distance would have them both seeing things more clearly.

Grannie and Aunt Tillie might figure that she was the one for him, but unless she felt the same, he would have to keep his hands to himself.

Holly Jane was a special woman. She deserved nothing but respect.

He'd respect the hell out of her until his mind put her clothes back on.

Last night he'd left Holly Jane on the back porch wrapped in nothing but his duster, then gone back out into the rain to gather up her clothing.

Life would be a damn sight simpler if he hadn't missed the camisole hanging on the elephant's trunk.

Grannie didn't miss it, though. First thing this morning she spotted it and trudged through the mud to see if she was hallucinating the merrily waving garment.

* * *

Holly Jane walked home from The Sweet Treat nibbling on a chocolate cookie.

"Did you know that my firstborn has a name, Lulu?" She stopped and peered down at the small pink pig while it stopped to snuffle at the bare branch of a wild rose. "It's Emily. Grannie Rose and Aunt Tillie have their hearts set on it."

It was a very good thing that Colt had moved into the barn because, as set on great-grandchildren as Grannie and Aunt Tillie were, Holly Jane was set on having a husband first.

She probably shouldn't have allowed Colt to touch her last night, but saying no would have been worse than pulling a tooth, worse than using salt in place of sugar...vinegar in place of honey.

The mystery of his touch would have been an itch in her heart. She would have always wondered.

And now she knew. Colt would be her man or no one would.

The idea of allowing another man to touch her the way he had was unthinkable. The thought of never being touched like that by him again was a knife to the heart.

This was proof that the old ladies' intuition had been spot-on from the very beginning.

Colt Wesson was her one and only. The trouble was he didn't know it yet.

Evidently he believed that she was virtue incarnate, while he was betrayer of everything good and respectable.

"I'd like to point out, Lulu, which one of us was sitting on the elephant naked last night."

Over breakfast this morning, Grannie Rose and Aunt Tillie had been tingling with joy over last night's events, which, because of her camisole, could not be hidden from them.

They assured her that Colt's moving into the barn was a very good sign. It meant he wanted to do the right thing by her.

If only she could believe that, her nerves might settle down. For all she knew, the reason he had moved into the barn was because he found her unappealing.

Tonight at dinner, she would ask the ladies not to speak of one and onlys.

He might dig in his heels and remind himself why she was not the one for him.

If there were an Emily then an Alexander in all of their futures, Colt could not be rushed.

She didn't know much about love, but what she did know, besides that she was in it, was that it couldn't be forced.

Love was like bread. It didn't just flash into being all at once. It required kneading and time to rise, time to be punched down then rise again.

Just because she had fallen in love in the blink of an eye, didn't mean that was normal.

Tonight, to relax and reassure herself that it would all work out well, she would bake bread.

Tomorrow morning she would take the loaf out to the barn. Colt wouldn't know that she was offering him time.

She would be patient, keep her clothes on no matter what and let the yeast do its work.

Holly Jane carried her loaf of bread and Colt's duster to the barn the next morning. The air was cold and crisp, a perfect start to the early-November day. In the east, the sky had just begun to turn red where the sun lit the belly side of a bank of clouds.

It should have been a peaceful moment, but she had the odd feeling that she ought to be looking over her shoulder. She hadn't felt that sensation since Colt had come to town and the Folsoms and the Broadhowers had given up on courting her.

She hugged her coat tighter about her shoulders and hurried inside through the small door.

Colt had set up his bed in an empty stall close to the big black stove that Granddaddy had installed. She hadn't seen it lit in several years. The warmth and the glow shot her back to the past, and it was not Colt, but Granddaddy that she saw filling the horse troughs with hay.

"Good morning," Holly Jane said to Colt, leaving the loaf of bread on the rail of the empty stall.

"Holly Jane." He nodded in her direction then went back to his work.

"It looks like a cold one today," she said, making her voice sound congenial. "You'll need your duster."

She hung it over the rail beside the bread.

He turned slowly then stuck the tines of his pitchfork into the stack of hay.

"About the other night—" he began, but she cut him off.

"It's best forgotten," she said quickly. She turned and walked toward Molly before he could read on her face that she would not forget a single detail of what happened the other night. When she was a wrinkled old woman she would be able to relive every second of that encounter.

She stroked Molly's nose, then turned toward the big barn door. Colt pushed it open to the fresh scent of the autumn morning. Clouds and sunshine battled for the day.

"Have a pleasant morning," she said brightly, stepping past him.

He caught her elbow. "Forgive me, Holly Jane."

She patted his hand. She smiled. "Really, Colt, there's no need. We're even, just like we said."

He let go of her elbow, and she backed away from him quickly before she did what she really wanted to and threw herself against his big, hard-muscled chest.

"Will we see you at dinner?" she asked, because it seemed like the polite thing to say. Like something she would say if he hadn't changed her world.

He answered with a frown.

By the time she reached the path through the woods, the birds had woken up. Sunlight kissed the treetops and reflected off the bare branches.

That uncomfortable sensation of being watched tingled again between her shoulder blades.

She glanced about quickly but saw nothing out of the ordinary.

Chances are she felt jittery because of the uneasy feelings between her and the man she had decided she could not live without.

"And don't forget," Holly Jane reminded Mrs. Henson, who walked out the door of The Sweet Treat with a dozen warm cookies in her basket, "the carousel will be running this Sunday after church. Bring your children and tell your neighbors."

The door opened and one of the Mrs. Broadhowers walked in.

"Thank you, Holly Jane," Mrs. Henson said. "And I'm so sorry you lost your grandfather's ranch the way you did. It was your home, after all."

"Oh, well. I didn't lose the whole thing. Granddaddy did leave me the land that the carousel is on."

"That's something, anyway. Maybe you can build yourself a little place and settle on it. We'll see you on Sunday afternoon."

Mrs. Henson waved goodbye but did not acknowledge Mrs. Broadhower.

"Good afternoon, Sylvie." Holly Jane smiled at her customer. "Can I help you with something?"

"That apple pie looks good. I'll take it."

Holly Jane lifted it from the display case and set it on the counter.

"Is it true, you didn't lose all the land?"

"I have the little bit that the carousel is on."

"It was a crime what your grandfather did to you."

What he did to the Broadhowers is more what she was probably thinking. Holly Jane didn't point that out, though, since her objective was peace, not contention.

"Mr. Travers has repaired the carousel. I'm inviting all the town children on Sunday afternoon. I'd be pleased to see you there."

"I imagine that wicked Mr. Travers will be there…and some Folsoms. There's bound to be trouble, Holly Jane. I think this is not a wise thing to do."

"Sylvie, don't you remember years ago when you brought your little brothers and sisters to the carousel? We all had so much fun."

"That was a long time ago. Things have changed."

"Just because you married a Broadhower doesn't mean you have to hate the Folsoms."

"Doesn't it? You are a single lady, Holly Jane. You wouldn't know anything about that." Sylvie Broadhower snatched her pie and left the shop.

As far as Holly Jane was concerned, Sylvie was as much a victim of the feud as anyone else. There was a time not many years ago when she had been a popular girl in town, known for her friendliness.

She turned toward the kitchen, ready to straighten up and go home, but another customer came in.

"How can I help you?" she asked the dusty-looking stranger.

"You Miss Holly Jane Munroe?" He removed his hat and gripped it in his fists. His fingernails were imbedded with grime. His hair looked like it hadn't seen a combing in some time.

"I am."

"I hear tell your treats are sweet." He stared at her then the case of pastries. "I'll have me a... whatever that thing is with the dots on it...for my long trip home."

Holly Jane took a scone from the case.

He snatched it up and started to walk out the door without paying for it. That would never do, tired traveler or not.

"That will be five cents, if you please."

"Sorry, ma'am." He dug in his pocket and drew out a nickel that he placed on the counter. "Ain't used to town ways."

"Have a safe trip home, sir," she said, and deposited the nickel in her apron pocket.

"It'll be a long weary ride but I reckon the trip will have been worth it, all in all."

As soon as he left the shop, she locked the door behind him and turned her thoughts to the coming evening.

Colt had taken his dinner in the barn last night. Grannie Rose was convinced that it had been because he would not to be able to resist her charms. Aunt Tillie figured it was because he was laden in shame.

In either case, they assured her, it boded well for the great-grandchildren.

Chapter Ten

Colt huddled into his duster against the brisk November wind. He turned up the collar. It was damn cold after sundown even wrapped up in his coat.

He stood in the yard watching the homey scene being played out through the dining room window. Holly Jane, Grannie Rose and Aunt Tillie sat about the table eating and laughing. Behind them he saw the flames of a cozy fire casting the dining room in a soft orange glow.

Only a fool would shiver outside, watching smoke curl out of the chimney. A boy might avoid going inside his own house because of a woman, but he hadn't been a boy in a long time. Hell, maybe he never had been.

He stomped up the porch stairs, strode through the parlor and into the dining room.

"Good evening, ladies." He shrugged out of his

coat and let the flames from the fireplace warm his backside. "What's on the menu?"

"It's good to see you've come to your senses, Colt." Aunt Tillie pointed to the place they had left for him at the table.

His dinner plate was already piled high with beef and spuds, so he sat down to the warm feast. He wouldn't miss supper in the barn. The horses hadn't turned out to be the most sociable of eating companions.

"We were just discussing what we should serve for the carousel party," Holly Jane said, smiling at him without a trace of resentment in her voice.

He nodded and shoved a spoon of potatoes in his mouth. It was almost as though she had forgotten the other night…or maybe that moment hadn't been the earthquake of passion for her that it had been for him.

"What do you think, Colt?" she asked. "Cookies are easier but pumpkin pies would suit the season."

He swallowed the lump of potatoes, hard.

"A chocolate pie would suit everyone, I'm sure." Grannie Rose smiled and patted his hand. "It might even sweeten your cousin Cyrus."

"We could send him one, I reckon," he said, and lightly pressed the tissue-thin flesh of her hand. "Doubt if it would get to the Broken Brand in one piece, though."

"But it wouldn't have to. Cyrus is here. I saw him just this morning."

"Here where, Grannie?" He was becoming alarmed by Grannie's visions. They seemed as real to her as Aunt Tillie's frown at this moment.

"He was at the carousel, sitting on the back of a giraffe…also in the garden, but that was later."

"It's a wonder he wasn't run off by the alligator, Rose," Aunt Tillie said with a sigh.

"The alligator wasn't there today, but the monkey was. He was hanging on to Cyrus's hat poking at his eyes. I did think it strange that Cyrus didn't seem to mind."

"Remember what we said, Rose? Those things you see aren't real. If the monkey really had been poking Cyrus in the eye, he'd have shot him."

"I don't recall a gunshot, and the monkey was fit as a fiddle just before dinner." Grannie Rose shrugged. "I'm still for chocolate-something… You decide, Holly Jane."

"How about chocolate cookies and pumpkin pie?"

"Seems to me the younglings might like some apple cider to keep them warm," Colt said.

"Or a hot toddy, heavy with chocolate and cream."

"All right, Grannie Rose," Holly Jane said. "Hot toddy for you, hot cider for Colt. We'll sweeten everyone with chocolate cookies and pumpkin pie."

"That ought to keep them all peaceable." Aunt Tillie nodded her approval.

"By the way, Colt," Grannie said, "you can move back into the house now. Your aunt Tillie and I have decided we were wrong. Holly Jane is not the one for you, after all."

"I reckon Holly Jane is relieved to hear it."

He glanced at Holly Jane to see what her reaction to this news would be. It was hard to tell; she wasn't looking at him. She was frowning at Grannie.

Just as well, since damn it, he didn't know what reaction he wanted from her.

If those brown eyes clouded in sorrow, he'd feel miserable. If they sparkled in relief, he'd feel worse.

That ought to tell him something, but he stuffed his belly rather than dwell upon it. The last thing he needed was his nosy relatives wondering what was on his mind.

Holly Jane flipped the sign on the door to Closed then walked across Town Square to Melinda's Ladies' Apparel. She hurried, helped along by the chilly wind.

Melinda, middle-aged, tall and slim, wore a white frilly apron over her dress. She stood over a trunk, lifting out gowns and shaking the wrinkles out of them.

She looked up when the bell over her door tinkled.

"Good afternoon, Holly Jane." Melinda wiped her hands on the apron. "I've been meaning to thank you. Your carousel party has certainly sent business my way."

"I hope there's a gown left for me." She had a new gown, tho pretty one that she had purchased in Homerville with Colt, but she wanted one that he had never seen her in.

"Luckily, I got a new shipment this morning." She dug through the trunk, pulled out a pink flowered dress, tossed it aside. Next, she pulled out a yellow one. "Yellow is your color, but I think something more... Here it is."

"I don't have anything red," Holly Jane admitted, thinking that the crimson garment was beautiful but bold.

"It's high time you did, miss. Hilde was in here yesterday trying on everything that would fit and some that wouldn't. She and her mother are set on stealing away that young man of yours."

"He not my young man to be stolen," Holly Jane protested, but weakly. The reason she was in the dress shop was to help make him her young man. "You think red would help?"

"Hilde insisted on a gray-blue one that she thought was a match to her eyes. She'll look like ice next to your fire, and no mistake about it."

"It is striking."

"Go in the fitting room and try it on. We'll see."

The gown covered her from the lace-edged neck to the ruffled hem, but it was the most alluring thing she had ever worn, even though it was wool.

"Oh, yes!" Melinda exclaimed, pacing a circle around her, "This was made for you. Besides, from what I've seen, Colt Travers would be bored silly by a woman in blue, no matter how immodest the bodice is."

She was probably right. Colt was far too dynamic a man to be attracted to anything as ordinary as washed-out blue. But there was the bodice to be considered. No doubt he had encountered many alluring ones over the years.

What she needed was to stand out…to be different than any woman he had ever met.

It would be red or nothing.

"I'm going to trust you, Melinda."

"I'll have this pressed and ready for you tomorrow afternoon."

Holly Jane stepped out of the dress shop, smiling. Come Sunday, she was going to be bold and flirtatious. Colt would not even know that Hilde was there. Not her nor any of the other pretty girls in town who had set their caps for the handsome new rancher in Friendship Springs.

Lulu waited for her on the front porch of The Sweet Treat, her corkscrew tail twitching.

"Come along then," Holly Jane called. "Let's go home."

Lulu trotted beside her on small pink feet, into the woods behind The Sweet Treat.

All of a sudden Holly Jane felt uncomfortable, like someone was watching her. It was the same strange sensation that had overcome her the other day. Even Lulu glanced into the brush, seeming anxious.

"Holly Jane," a man's voice spoke from behind. She spun about, but it was only Henry Broadhower.

"My word, Henry, you startled me."

"Could be that's a good thing. Time's up for you to be turning down every Broadhower who proposes." Henry puffed out his chest, looking like a bristling porcupine. "This is the last time you'll get a peaceable offer of marriage."

"I hope it is the last time. You know that Colt Travers owns Granddaddy's land now, not me."

"That's what he told folks, but you still own some of it. That property could be what keeps the water flowing to our land."

"You and the Folsoms are just the same, seeing trouble everywhere. Mr. Travers isn't going to do a thing to your water."

"He might not, but if one of those pigheaded Folsoms gets a hold of you, there's going to be a bloodbath."

"No one is going to get a hold of me."

"I'm done asking." He yanked her to him with a wide fist around her arm. "You'll marry me no matter what I have to do to get it done… You understand my meaning, Holly Jane?"

She kicked his shin. Lulu, as small as she was had razor-sharp teeth. She used them to nip Henry's ankle.

He let out a bellow and balled up his fist, ready to swing a blow at her face. All of a sudden a rock hit the back of his head. Henry dropped to the dirt, moaning.

Shrubbery rustled. Footsteps pounded the earth, running away. She couldn't see who her rescuer was.

Lulu dashed toward home on her short, quick legs. Holly Jane tried to keep up, but with only two legs, she wasn't as swift.

As if announcing the danger, Lulu squealed her piggy lungs out.

Colt paused, his pitchfork halfway into a scoop of hay when he heard Lulu's caterwauling. The little porker sounded like the devil was trying to steal her twirly-gig tail.

He rushed out past the big barn door carrying his pitchfork with him.

What the hell? Holly Jane and her little pig ran across the bridge, skirts and cleft feet flying.

He dropped the fork and ran toward her, his fingers reaching for the hilt of the toothpick.

"Get back inside the house!" he yelled at Grannie and Aunt Tillie who had come outside to investigate the commotion.

Aunt Tillie grabbed Grannie's hand and they hurried down the front steps.

He caught Holly Jane to him a hundred yards from the barn. She could have dashed for the safety of the house, but she'd run to him instead.

That stirred something in him. It made him want to claim her, make her his to defend.

"What is it?" He stroked her back, trying to soothe her labored breathing.

Aunt Tillie snatched up Lulu and rushed her to the water pump.

"There's someone in the woods," she gasped. "Throwing rocks."

"At you?" he wanted to shout, but he said it as gently as his anger would allow.

She pushed away from his chest with both hands. She shook her head.

"At Henry Broadhower."

His anger, which had begun to calm, seeing that Holly Jane was not injured or the target of the rock thrower, roared back to life.

"You were alone in the woods with Broadhower?"

"Well, no… There was the person who hit him with the rock."

He hadn't noticed Grannie standing close by until she spoke. "Cyrus always was a rock thrower. Even Tillie's cane couldn't make him quit."

"He could hardly have thrown a rock from the Broken Brand, Rose," Aunt Tillie pointed out.

"Not with the monkey poking him in the eye, at least."

"Why don't you ladies take Lulu in the house and give her a treat while I speak with Holly Jane."

Grannie looked as though she wanted to say something, but Aunt Tillie shoved Lulu into her arms and hustled her toward the house.

Wind rushed across the ground. Holly Jane shivered. He led her into the barn and settled her on a saddle draped over a sawhorse.

"What was it Broadhower wanted?" He plucked his duster from a stall gate and tucked it across her shoulders.

"The usual." She clasped the lapels of his coat together. Her fingers weren't shivering any longer. "But this time he wasn't asking, he was demanding. He threatened—"

Colt cussed, and this time not under his breath.

"Henry found out that I still own the carousel land and figures if a Folsom gets a hold of it before a Broadhower does, they'll cut off the water to the Broadhower land. It's the same old thing, except that he would have dragged me to the preacher if someone hadn't hit him on the head with a rock."

Dragging Holly Jane to the preacher was probably not what Broadhower had in mind. More likely he had compromise on his mind.

He cursed again, but this time under his breath so as not to alarm Holly Jane.

"Did you see who threw the rock?"

"No."

"A Folsom, more likely than not." He straddled the end of the sawhorse and sat down. "We need to call off the carousel party. There's bound to be trouble."

"I won't call it off. If there's to be any hope for Friendship Springs, it has got to be through the children."

Colt crossed his arms over his chest and took a slow, patience-gathering breath. He didn't like it that she was right.

"I agree with you… Don't damn like it, though."

"We'll just have to be wary." Holly Jane stood up. She shrugged out of his coat and handed to him. "See you at supper."

"Sell me the carousel land."

That would finally keep her safe from both families. He wouldn't have to maim anybody, either.

She turned at the small barn door, holding it open to the sunset.

"It's all I have."

"I reckon you could marry me. That would keep you safe."

Moisture dampened her eyes all of a sudden. She shook her head then stepped outside and closed the door behind her.

What the hell had possessed him to say that? As proposals went it was garbage. A woman like Holly Jane deserved to be wooed and courted.

She needed a gentle man, one who was as respectable as a preacher on Sunday.

Holly Jane came downstairs in her red dress at noon on Sunday. With the scent of snow in the air, she was grateful for the high neckline and the warm fabric. She looked out the window. It was cloudy, but with any luck the weather would hold off until the party was over.

So much work had gone into the preparation that she would turn on the carousel even if there were a blizzard and she and the ladies the only ones to enjoy it.

Last night, she and Colt had worked until late in the evening getting the barn ready. They'd made a table of sawhorses and an old door. Planks of lumber had been fashioned into benches.

Things had seemed easy between them, but only in the way that a still surface covered agitated waters. It had cut her to the quick when he had asked her to marry him. No "I love you…be mine," not even a "we could be so happy."

To him it was a solution to a problem.

She did not intend to be a problem; she intended to be a blessing. It took most of the night to get her emotions in order, but today was a new day.

Today, Colt Wesson would learn that she was not only helpful, dependable and a good cook, but more seductive than any woman he had ever hankered for.

Decked out in her new crimson gown, she felt like forbidden fruit, fresh and succulent.

She picked up a tray of cookies and a pie then carried them out of the house, past the carousel and toward the barn. Cold air nipped her skin through the dress, but she was not going to cover the pretty garment with a drab coat.

She nudged the small barn door open with her hip. Welcome warmth wrapped her up the instant she stepped inside.

She set the tray of cookies and the pie on the table.

"Colt?" she called into the softly lit barn.

He didn't answer. She wouldn't blame him if he'd gone to his stall and fallen asleep. He'd worked far later than she had getting the barn warm and ready for the party.

She knew it because she had been watching the barn from her bedroom window. All right, mooning at it more than watching, but it had been 3:10 a.m. when the lamps had gone out.

"Colt?" she called again.

This time she heard a soft brushing sound coming from an empty stall in the back corner.

She found him sitting on a stool, drawing the length of his long knife against a leather strop hanging from the wall.

It glinted in the lantern light, sliding back and forth over the leather with a lethal hiss.

He looked up at her, grinning. "You ready for the big shindig, for everybody to make friends?"

"That's what I'm counting on." She walked up close to him and touched his wrist, stilling the swipe of the blade. "Colt, can't you leave that thing here?"

"Wouldn't be smart, Sunshine, not with the Folsoms and the Broadhowers within punching distance of each other."

"I'm sure you're right, but the children need to be considered before anything else."

"It's their safety I've got in mind." He stood up,

sheathed the knife and hung it on a wall peg. "But it's your party."

She wanted to kiss him. All she would have to do is step forward two steps, rise up on her toes and cup his jaw in her hands, then stake her claim.

If only capturing a man's love were as easy as that.

Colt Wesson was not the kind of man to be taken so simply. All she could do was wait for him to see what was right in front of his face…really, only a few inches away.

Waiting would take a good deal of patience this afternoon, with Hilde in her low-cut gown going after him like a frog after a fly.

And not just Hilde… She imagined that a few women in town were looking in boudoir mirrors, arranging curls, pinching their cheeks pink and practicing flirtatious smiles.

Well—she shook herself—they were not her concern at the moment. Bringing peace to Friendship Springs by way of the children was the main thing that mattered this afternoon.

"You cold, Holly Jane?" Colt rubbed her upper arms briskly with his big calloused hands.

She shook her head. "Just a little anxious about how things will go today."

"I can bring the Toothpick." Both dimples creased with his grin.

"I can't hold a friendly get-together if you're going to carve up the first guest who gets out of line."

The sound of buggy wheels crossing the bridge made her stomach flip. This would be the second step toward Friendship Springs becoming the peaceable place to live that most of the citizens longed for. The first had been the Folsom and the Broadhower girls meeting at The Sweet Treat.

If they came today, would they associate with each other openly?

She straightened her shoulders and turned toward the small barn door.

Colt touched her elbow and spun her back to face him.

"You look beautiful, Holly Jane." He touched her cheek with the work-roughened skin of his knuckles. "Let's go make this town a friendly place to live."

It didn't set well, leaving his blade in the barn. Tingles crawled along the back of his neck, a warning that, in spite of the pretty scene going on all around him, something wasn't right.

Children rode the carousel; they ran about playing tag while their mothers sipped warm drinks and gossiped.

Even though this was an event for children, for making friends and bringing peace, Colt worried that all the sugar in the county would not make some of the folks sweet.

So far, none of the sour souls had shown up. Things seemed to be going along just like Holly Jane hoped they would.

He kept a guarded eye on the folks having fun, hoping that nothing would change.

"Aren't the children so sweet that you could eat them up?" came a feminine voice from behind him.

The young woman walked boldly up and stood closer to him than, he figured, her folks would be happy with.

"Miss Munroe made some cookies so you won't have to do that."

He took a wide step away from her, but she filled it in with a swish of her pink skirt.

"I just adore children, don't you?" She blinked her eyes at him, fast and hard. He reckoned she had spent some time practicing the flirtation. "Of course you do. You wouldn't invite them to your beautiful ranch if that weren't the case."

She slipped her arm through his and clamped on hard. Clearly, she wasn't refined in the art of seduction, but she was eager.

"I want a houseful of the little dears." She sighed and looked him in the eye. "Given all this, I don't doubt that you want the same."

"This is all Holly Jane's doing," he explained, pretending to misunderstand what she was suggesting.

The woman was curvy where a woman ought to be, her face was pretty and she would take a tumble as easily as a pebble on a slope.

At one time he would have felt a response to her promiscuous behavior. Not now. It wasn't right that he didn't even know her name, yet she clung to him like tar on a feather.

Unless he missed his guess, she saw him as the daddy of her brood.

"Holly Jane is a dear little thing," the woman said, her voice ripe with dismissal.

"The lady has spunk…and beauty." He watched Holly Jane in the distance. His heart swelled with pride as though she were his in some way. "She's a rare one, wouldn't you agree?"

"Well," the woman blustered, "she is sweet-tempered."

Colt watched Holly Jane lift a little boy up on a wooden horse. They laughed and she patted his head.

She glanced about and spotted him with Nameless stuck to his arm. With a laugh, she climbed on the elephant's back.

She smiled, she winked. He felt a surge of heat roar through his limbs.

Holly Jane was dearer than Nameless could imagine. She was also smart, brave and caring…not to mention as spicy as her modest, but somehow provocative, red dress.

He was going to tell her so. If she rejected him, so be it. He could not face the rest of his life without offering his heart.

It was worth the risk. If she did feel the same for him as he felt for her, he would gain the world. If she didn't, hell and damn

The pressure of fingers trailing up his sleeve brought his attention back to the woman attached to him.

"Ma'am?" He uncurled her fingers from the crook of his arm. "I believe my grandmother needs me."

It might be true. Where was the old gal anyway? The last time he had seen her she was riding a fish on the carousel and chomping down a chocolate cookie. That had to have been half an hour ago.

He hurried to the carousel, jumped upon it then walked into the spin. Passing the grinning little boy, he stopped at the elephant and rested his hand on the tip of the trunk that had held Holly Jane's camisole.

She looked pretty sitting astride the wooden beast with her red skirt splayed over the animal's rump, but she might as well have not gotten dressed for all that he saw of her gown. There would never be a day when he didn't see her sitting backward, naked and sighing under his touch.

"Have you seen Grannie?" he asked, in part as a reminder that this was now and not then. The women in his life were expecting him to act like a gentleman this afternoon.

A pair of creases wrinkled her brow.

"Not since she went into the barn for more sweets. I hope she hasn't taken ill." She lifted her leg over the elephant's back, ready to climb down. "I'll go look in the house."

He caught her waist to ease her descent. Anyone

would think so. The truth was that he wanted to touch her…to feel the warmth and the life inside her.

Since he'd moved into the barn, things hadn't been the same. Even with his dream of raising horses on his own land being fulfilled on an hourly basis, something was missing.

Didn't take much wondering to know what it was.

Joy in the form of Holly Jane. It was sharing common moments with her. Watching her laugh with the old ladies at the dining table. Hearing her talk to her pig when she thought he wasn't nearby. Seeing moonlight tickle soft fingers through her sleeping gown when she went out late at night to visit the outhouse.

The fact that he was in love couldn't be clearer if Cupid were stinging him with an arrow.

"There she is." Holly Jane patted his hands where he'd neglected to remove them from her waist. "See her coming around the back of the house?"

"There's something I need to…" His confession trailed off because all of a sudden her face lit up, and it wasn't because of him.

"It's the girls!" She hopped off the moving platform to greet the new guests.

He ought to go back into the barn and get his knife, because three Folsom girls had just crossed the bridge, arm in arm with four Broadhower girls.

Chapter Eleven

"Miss Munroe!" Susan waved at her from the bridge.

The girl bounced on her toes, gesturing to her friends and relatives to hurry.

They rushed toward the carousel, laughing and clapping their hands.

"This is so beautiful!" Cissy Broadhower exclaimed, her cheeks flushed pink with excitement and a nip of cold. "I can't believe such a thing exits."

"We'd heard the stories about how it used to be, but I never quite believed them," Bethanne said.

As excited as the girls were, Holly Jane was jubilant…ready to weep, in fact, because Bethanne snatched Cissy's hand and they ran to the carousel as though they had always been best friends. Even better, they always would be.

"Go on, girls," Holly Jane said to the others. "Better get some riding done before it starts to snow."

Laughter trailed after the girls like a ribbon of joy wrapping everyone in its bow.

Sarah Milton whispered in Ellie Landers's ear. They giggled then approached Bethanne and Cissy.

While she watched, children from other families appeared to overcome their fear of the Broadhowers and the Folsoms.

If the yard weren't filled with folks of all ages munching sweets and having fun, Holly Jane would dissolve into a weeping mess of happy tears. A few months ago she would never have believed that peace would be possible for the town.

Now, because of Colt repairing the carousel, there was hope. If she had it to do over again, she would not have greeted him and his family with a disheveled home.

"Wouldn't have believed it," Colt's voice said, surprising her from behind. She'd been so involved in watching the children that she hadn't noticed him approach.

"I wonder if Granddaddy can see this," she said.

"I reckon he can." Colt stood so close that his breath stirred the hair at her temple. "Close your eyes…see if you can't feel him."

With her eyes closed, she noticed things she wouldn't have. A note in the tune of the carousel's song off-key. A woman's voice that laughed a bit louder than the drone of conversation. The scent of apple cider drifting from the barn, the cold nip of the air promising snowfall before dark, and there, close beside her, she sensed Granddaddy's presence.

If she dared to open her eyes she might see him standing beside Colt, grinning and clapping him on the back. Couldn't she just hear him if she listened with her heart, telling Colt he was pleased that he was bringing the ranch back, thanking him that his granddaughter was not married to a Folsom or a Broadhower?

She startled, because she felt her grandfather turn his attention to her.

"Emily." She heard his voice in her mind as clearly as when he had stood beside her in the flesh. "Or Alexander. Your grandma says to tell you she loves you and don't dawdle on those babies."

She heard the laugh that she missed every day since Granddaddy had gone.

Her visit ended abruptly when another laugh intruded.

"My word, Mr. Travers. I'm such a ninny, leaving my coat behind." Hilde shivered. Her flesh pebbled where the bodice of her gown dipped too low to offer anything but a clear view of her charms. "I'm as cold as can be."

"No need to be cold, Hilde," Holly Jane said, still feeling Granddaddy at her back, urging her to fight for little Emily and baby Alexander. "The barn's plenty warm and the cider is hot."

"I'm sure it is, Holly Jane." Hilde turned around,

presenting her back. Holly Jane felt like an intruder on a private conversation.

"Maybe I could bring you my coat from the house."

"Yes," she said, turning at the waist and spearing her with a vinegar smile. "Be a dear, won't you?"

"Mr. Travers." Hilde turned back to Colt, the vinegar vanished, drippy honey taking its place. "I'd so adore a ride on the carousel with you. Won't you please go around with me on the elephant?"

"Thing is, Goose Bump, I had my heart set on riding the elephant with Holly Jane." He reached around Hilde to snatch Holly Jane's hand. "Best go warm up with some cider."

Holly Jane laughed. It wasn't kind, but she couldn't help it.

Hilde had been so sure of herself, of the charm of her low-cut gown, and now all she got for her effort was the shivers.

Colt Wesson had been her hero from the beginning, standing between her and her suitors. Today, he was that and more.

Hilde had made her feel like a child…a nuisance.

With a wink and a smile, Colt had chosen her… in front of Hilde and anyone else who might have been witnessing her humiliation.

She would love him forever.

With her chilly hand wrapped up in his big, warm

one, he ran with her to the carousel. He lifted her up, turning her backward on the elephant. Just like before, he climbed on and faced her.

"Thank you, Colt. It was kind—"

He touched her cheek. "No one makes you feel small, Holly Jane."

He traced her lips with his thumb. He kissed her gently just as the carousel rounded upon an outraged Hilde, who had been joined by her equally stunned mother.

"Meet me here tonight." He cupped the back of her head with his hand. "There's some things I have to say to you, and I won't do it with all these damned eyes staring at us."

"I'll be here, as soon as the ladies are in bed."

A gust of wind carried a snowflake that settled on the corner of his grin, then another on his hair. He slipped off the elephant then rested his hand on her thigh.

"I won't be riding the elephant with anyone but you ever again."

He squeezed her knee then jumped from the moving platform. Passing by Hilde and her mother without a glance, he turned and winked, then went into the barn.

Nothing would keep her from being here tonight, not a blizzard, a flood, or a pair of old ladies wanting to sit up late and talk.

For a brief second he was there. Granddaddy, riding the horse next to her, nodding his approval.

* * *

Colt watched Goose Bumps cross the bridge, her gray-blue skirt swaying with her angry stride. The vapor of her mother's breath trailed behind while she tried to keep pace with her daughter.

There had been a time, all of his life to be honest, that he would have followed her…a full-bosomed, earthy and slightly lacking in morals, siren. The kind of woman who accepted a man like him without a qualm.

This afternoon he had sent her on her way without regret.

It seemed that his type had become the kind of woman who was as beautiful on the inside as she was on the outside. When the two qualities were bound up in one little lady wearing a modest, but all the more alluring for it, dress, she was irresistible.

She would be his.

Holly Jane went from guest to guest, carrying a tray of cookies and pie. She walked through the intermittent snowflakes, looking like some sort of Fairy princess seeing to the sweet needs of her kingdom.

He'd have to stay away from her, keep his hands on proper things until folks went home. But come tonight, he wouldn't.

He dodged a pair of running children then went into the barn. The stove would need feeding.

Grannie and Aunt Tillie sat on the bench near

the stove. Aunt Tillie sipped something from a mug while Grannie dipped a cookie in her hot drink.

He sat down beside them.

"Holly Jane must be pleased," Aunt Tillie said, nodding her head toward the group of girls in the corner. "There's got to be ten of them now, Folsoms and Broadhowers, even some other girls from town."

"I'd like to be young like that again, wouldn't you, sister?"

"If only to try harder to talk you out of running away with an outlaw."

"Luckily, I wouldn't have paid a blink of attention. We wouldn't have had our little Colt if I had. If there were no Colt, what would become of Emily and Alexander?"

"Grannie." Colt folded her splotched and veined hand in his. He thought her hand was beautiful with its lines that revealed a lifetime. "You know that Emily and Alexander don't exist?"

She sighed. "Yes, dear, and Cyrus wasn't just behind the house with the monkey and the alligator, either."

"Colt—" Aunt Tillie touched his back "—you aren't wearing your sword today."

"First of all it's not a sword."

"It might as well be," Grannie observed. "And we haven't seen you without it in years."

"Holly Jane didn't think it was right wearing it around the children. It's hanging in the back stall."

He hadn't gotten used to the feeling of being

without it. He felt vulnerable, what with the buzz of unease in his gut that wouldn't let up and not a damn thing he could do if something happened.

"That ought to tell you something about your feelings for Holly Jane, young man." Judging by their matching expressions, Aunt Tillie spoke for the both of them.

"Tells me I'll probably be sorry."

At that moment Holly Jane came through the barn door with a light flurry of snowflakes rushing in with her. He reckoned that folks wouldn't be staying much longer.

Holly Jane walked to the pot of apple cider and dipped the ladle in. She turned to him and raised her mug.

Until tonight, was her clear message. Good thing he wasn't holding a cup of something hot or he'd have sloshed it all over his fingers.

He'd need his fingers later on. Damned if they weren't itching in anticipation of slowly stripping that red dress off her.

Susan Broadhower nibbled on her fingernail. Bethanne Folsom yanked her friend's hand from her mouth and held it.

"Things are different for us, Suzie." Bethanne shook her head. "It's not right or fair, but it's a born-and-bred fact."

Susan turned to Holly Jane on the bench. "Shouldn't I be able to court a Folsom if I want to?"

Holly Jane glanced out the barn door, watching the snow drift softly past. Sadly, she couldn't give the girl the answer she wanted.

"You're too young for courting just yet," she answered then took a sip of her cider and let the warm liquid glide down her throat while she searched her heart for a bit of wisdom to give the child. "All of you are the hope for this town. Old ways won't last forever. Keep on doing what you are, meeting and bringing in more friends. With any luck, Suzie… and the rest of you, will be able to court anyone you choose to."

"I'd choose to court Mr. Travers," a pigtailed girl, who was neither a Folsom nor a Broadhower, said with a sigh. "But I'm thirteen. He'll be an old man by the time I'm even old enough to be noticed."

"Well, we'd all court him, Clara, but he's Miss Munroe's fellow," Bethanne pointed out.

He wasn't, but come later tonight he might be. She glanced about the barn but didn't see him.

"I saw him go out with his grannie and his aunt a few minutes ago." Clara twirled the tip of her pigtail about her finger.

"The snow's getting heavier. I reckon we ought to go home like the rest of the folks have," Susan said.

"But it's so dreary. Uncle Henry is going to go on talking about how we will all come to ruin if a Folsom grabs Miss Munroe first. And the threats against Mr. Travers. It's all we ever hear," Cissy complained.

"I'm not going to be grabbed by anyone. Tell your families they don't have to worry about their water. Colt has no intention of drying anyone out."

"Be careful, Miss Munroe." Bethanne's pretty face looked weighed down with worry. "Our grandfather found out that Henry Broadhower has decided to cart you off, willing or not. Now he's trying to get one of my uncles to do it first."

"Since we all saw Mr. Travers kiss you today, we reckon he ought to marry you as soon as he can," Clara said.

"That ought to get both of our families into a tangle. I really don't want to go home," Cissy moaned.

"You bunch of worthless, disloyal females! I figured I'd find you here!" A big, booming voice rang off the walls. The horses that Colt had brought in when the snow started falling stomped nervously in their stalls. "Stand up, you Broadhower girls! I'm going to tan you right here for everyone to see your shame."

"No, Uncle Henry!" Susan rushed forward, placing her slight body between him and the other girls.

Henry Broadhower shoved her aside, not seeming to care that he had thrown her into a stall door. Susan cried out in pain and grabbed her shoulder.

"Henry Broadhower, get out of my barn." Holly Jane rushed him. It was a foolish thing to do, the man was three times her size, but he could not be allowed to threaten children.

He made a wide, balled-up swipe at her, but she ducked beneath his fist.

"Ain't your barn no more," he snarled.

Out of the corner of her eye she saw Bethanne rush to Susan. She knelt beside her friend, holding and rocking her while she wept.

"Folsom girl, get back to your own kind."

"Or what?" Holly Jane stood in front of both girls, presenting a frail barrier between them and Henry. "You'll throw little Bethanne against the barn wall, too?"

"I'll hang her from the rafters by her dirty bloomers!" His ugly laugh pounded off the roof.

The other children fled the barn, crying.

"Here's an idea," he barked.

He came toe-to-toe with her, so close that she could see the fine red veins in his bulbous nose as he stared her down. As much as she wanted to run for Colt, she couldn't. One step to the left or right would give him a clear path to the girls.

"You leave with me…we visit the preacher, and I don't do a single thing to reprimand the girls."

"Don't do it, Miss Munroe," Susan gritted through her pain.

"Here's a better idea, Sap Head. You don't reprimand the girls and I won't kill you."

Henry spun about. With his attention distracted, Holly Jane hurried to the girls and grabbed a pitchfork leaning on the inside of the stall.

Why had she insisted that Colt go without his

weapon? It had been foolish. Now it might be up to her to fend off this crazy Broadhower with a rusty tool. She wasn't certain she had the strength.

"How you aim to do that, seein' as you ain't armed?"

"I'm smarter than you are." Colt walked in a circle; Broadhower pivoted, following his movement. Colt stopped when he had positioned himself between her and Broadhower. "Stronger, too."

From behind, she watched Colt's posture begin to subtly change. He was going to attack, but his enemy was blustering too pompously to notice.

"Too bad for you." Henry reached into his pocket. "I brought my sidearm."

Colt sprang. He grabbed Broadhower at the knees. The big man tumbled backward and hit his head on the barn floor. Colt dived on top of him, with a knee to his groin. He snatched the gun from Henry's fist.

"Too bad for you, you're stupid." Colt extended the gun to her. "Dump this in the water trough, Sunshine."

Holly Jane dropped the pitchfork and grabbed the gun. She held it away from her and hurried to the trough. The gun gurgled through the water then hit the bottom with a thunk.

Henry shoved Colt off him then lumbered to his feet. What the man couldn't see, and Holly Jane could, was Colt's grin.

He snarled and lunged, but Colt caught his arm,

yanked it behind him and slammed Henry into the barn wall.

The snap of bone made her cringe.

"Looks like you broke your shoulder, Slim." Colt took a position between Henry and the girls. "If I were you I'd get on home. Make sure you've got water running through your place in the morning."

Henry stumbled out of the barn, his yowl screeching until the woods absorbed the sound.

Colt stooped down and inspected Susan's shoulder.

"Don't think it's broken, miss, but we better have the doc take a look at it." He gathered her gently in his arms and stood up.

"I'm going with you," Holly Jane said.

"Grannie and Aunt Tillie are uneasy. Will you stay and see to them for me?"

She nodded.

He set off toward town carrying Susan because it would be gentler than riding a horse. Bethanne walked beside them, gazing up at Colt like she was falling in love.

Well, Holly Jane sighed, closing the barn door then walking back toward the house, *who wouldn't fall in love with him?*

Colt walked around the edge of the carousel platform. The echo of his boots striking wood was muted by the curtain of snowfall drifting past the roof.

The lamps in the house had flickered out an hour ago.

If Holly Jane were coming, she ought to have been here by now.

He huddled into his duster and stared at her bedroom window.

He couldn't blame her for not showing. He was a rough man, sometimes violent. She had witnessed that firsthand a few hours ago.

Maybe he shouldn't have said that thing about not riding the elephant. It must have pushed her away.

Hell, she was probably shivering in her bed for fear of him. Being sweet and gentle like she was, she wouldn't understand that there were men in the world who didn't respect anything but a strong hand.

The fact that he'd simply given Broadhower a broken shoulder showed his restraint. The man deserved to have all his bones broken for the way he had treated his niece.

Colt had carried Susan to town as carefully as though he were toting a bag of eggs. The pain in her shoulder had to be intense, but she hadn't cried out over it.

The same couldn't be said of her uncle, who had gotten to the doctor ahead of them and wailed his lungs out while his shoulder was set.

It worried him that Holly Jane had not even come out to find out what had become of Susan. She might at least have met him on the porch.

As it turned out, the girl would be black-and-blue for a good long time, but as far as the doc could see, nothing had been broken. The doc and his wife had insisted that she spend the night with them, or forever, depending upon how long it took Henry Broadhower to become halfway reasonable.

Colt waited, shivering under his coat for another half hour before he figured that Holly Jane was not going to meet him.

Couldn't blame her, really. The rough side of him had been let loose this afternoon. As necessary as that had been, it made him feel dirty...cursed by his bloodline.

Chances are, Holly Jane had not shown up because she'd seen a man she didn't want.

Colt decided two things during the night. One was that the barn was too cold for a human to sleep in when he had a perfectly good bedroom in the house.

The other was that he was going to talk to Grannie and Aunt Tillie and find out what to do about Holly Jane. He meant to plead his case to her and those wise old women might know how to go about it better than he did.

He came inside through the kitchen mudroom, dusting the snow from his hat and stomping it from his boots.

The scent of flapjacks and melted butter greeted him. So did Lulu. Her small feet tapped across the kitchen floor. She chuffed at his boots then nipped his pant leg. The pig tried to yank his leg toward the back door.

The animal's behavior was odd. So was the fact that she was still here. Normally, she would have accompanied Holly Jane to The Sweet Treat.

It was unusual for Holly Jane to stay home from work, no matter what the weather. She was dedicated to buying back the ranch; she never let a foul day stand in the way of earning the next dollar toward that cause…as futile as the cause was.

"Hey, Bacon, let loose or you'll pay for the mending." He reached for the pig but she scuttled to the back door and sat down in front of it. She grunted.

"Holly Jane sick?" he asked as if the animal could understand him. To give the porker her due, she was a smart critter and seemed to understand when Holly Jane spoke to her. "Is that why she didn't go to work?"

Or show up at the carousel?

He found Grannie and Aunt Tillie sitting at the dining table.

"You seen Holly Jane?"

"Not since bedtime." Aunt Tillie set down the knife she had just dipped in a pot of honey. "I heard the door close late, but I assumed she went to meet you."

Colt turned toward the hall with Lulu trotting beside him. He took the stairs two at time.

He knocked on Holly Jane's closed door.

Silence… No rustling of bedclothes, no even rise and fall of breathing to indicate that she was sleeping.

Fear began a slow cramp in his belly.

Broadhower had been in no condition to take her the way he had threatened to, but what about one of the Folsoms? They wanted Holly Jane, too.

He opened the door. A sleeping gown lay across the bed, fresh and unused.

"I don't believe she slept in her bed last night," Grannie observed.

"Maybe she's at The Sweet Treat." Aunt Tillie went to the window, pulled aside the curtain and looked out. "The snow isn't too deep."

Colt crossed to the wardrobe and yanked the door open. "If she did, she was wearing the same dress as yesterday. It's not in here."

Blood swelled in his veins, hot and angry. It thudded in his ears; it sounded like a drum…a war drum. There might be a Folsom or a Broadhower who wouldn't see a healthy sundown.

"Must have been Cyrus, after all," Grannie said. "He told me to tell you that you can have her back when you take your rightful place in the family."

"Cyrus was here?" Colt spoke gently to Grannie, even though his temper had him needing to shout.

"I said so, I'm sure, only yesterday."

"But we thought…" Aunt Tillie sat down hard on the bed. "With the alligator and the monkey… I'm sorry, Rose… I thought Cyrus was the same."

"I should have listened to you, Grannie. I'm damn sorry I didn't." He lifted her hand and kissed it. "Is there anything else you can tell us?"

"Well, she'll be safe from the Folsoms and the Broadhowers for the time being."

"And we know where he is taking her," Aunt Tillie said.

To the Broken Brand…a ranch just this side of Hell.

Chapter Twelve

Poor Colt...poor little boy, was the only thing that Holly Jane could think of when she saw the Broken Brand in the distance. Knowing what he had gone through as a child in this place made it look all the more miserable.

She sat on one of the horses that Cyrus Travers had stolen from behind a saloon in Brownsite, Nebraska and wanted to weep for the first time since Colt's cousin had snatched her on her way to the outhouse.

How this collection of ramshackle sheds could have produced a man like Colt was hard to imagine.

"Almost home, Miss Munroe." Cyrus's stale breath fouled the air, even from a distance of five feet. "Once Colt Wesson marries you, you'll be queen of all this."

"What if he doesn't come?" She breathed in shallow breaths hoping that he would turn his face away.

"I was watching when you didn't notice. I saw how things were. Wouldn't have gone to the trouble of escorting you here if that weren't true."

Escorting was not quite the word she would have used. He had overcome her by locking his arm around her neck and squeezing until she passed out.

She had come to in the back of a buckboard. When she tried to climb out, he'd done it to her again.

At one point she'd heard him telling someone that his wife was asleep in back, ailing with the monthlies.

She'd struggled to rise from the splintered bed but her head felt like it weighed a hundred pounds. Judging by the nasty taste in her mouth she suspected she'd been drugged with some disgusting brew.

She hadn't been able to tell how much time passed since she'd been aware of anything, but it seemed to be early afternoon. As her mind had cleared, one thing had become perfectly apparent...she had no idea where she was. She might try to escape, but what would come of it? She had no money, no means of getting anywhere, even if she knew where it was she ought to get to.

There was only one hope...that Colt would come for her. While she didn't know where she was, he very likely did.

Her best chance of getting home was to stay with Cyrus, so she had crossed miles of desolate land without a struggle.

"He left this place behind," she said. "He won't come."

"I've picked my bait well. He'll come." Cyrus scratched his ear.

"Why do you want him back so bad when he doesn't want to be here?"

"It's his obligation. As Pappy Travers's only son, it's his place…and yourn'."

"My place is in Friendship Springs."

"Not anymore, it ain't. You're the bride, kidnapped good and proper. Nearly so, leastwise. Ought to have been my cousin took you, himself." He looked at her with a frown. "Doesn't make any sense why you would want to stay there and be snatched up by that big Broadhower fellow. My cousin has his shortcomings and I won't deny it, but he's a better choice."

"It was you who hit Henry with the rock?"

"Couldn't very well let him take you when I meant to do it myself."

"Thank you, Cyrus…I think."

"No need to. Once my cousin marries you and takes his place as leader, I'll be bound to do whatever you say."

"Why?"

What would make him say such a thing?

"Haven't you got ears, girl? Blood obligation—that's what this whole thing has been about from the get-go. Some's obliged to lead, some's obliged to follow."

"What happens if he doesn't marry me and take his place?"

"I won't have any cause to see to your safety." He looked at her, his expression hard. In his stare she saw that a lifetime of crime had snuffed out the man's moral fiber, had there been any to begin with. "Better hope he comes."

An hour later they reined up in front of a building that looked like it wouldn't last through the winter.

A woman came out of the house to stand on the slanted porch, her hands fisted on her hips and her smile as welcoming as a rattlesnake's. Old clothing hung from her shoulders, the color washed out of the fabric long ago.

"This is what you brought back, brother?" The woman approached her. She came close and fingered the hem of Holly Jane's warm wool skirt.

"Her and the horses." Cyrus dismounted and strode over to the woman, the leather of his boots squeaking as he walked.

"Like to see her last the winter."

"She don't have to, Edith, just long enough to bring Colt home."

"We don't need him. He never was a Travers worthy of the name." She yanked on Holly Jane's hem. "Get down off the horse so we can see to its care."

Holly Jane dismounted, stroking the animal's jaw and whispering in its ear. With a snort, it nuzzled her ribs. The poor thing probably missed home. It would be a shame to see the creature become as skinny and swaybacked as the few standing list-lessly in the corral.

Frigid wind blew over the land. It caught her skirt, swirled it up to reveal her lacy petticoat.

Edith's eyes widened for a second, then hardened.

"You'll be staying over there." She nodded her head at what, in kindly terms, could be called a shed.

The splintered building was all the way on the far side of the corral. At best it would keep out some of the wind.

"Well, get moving." Edith nudged her with an elbow in the back. "I don't have all day to socialize."

Holly Jane walked toward the shed, wondering if this was the same building from which Colt used to free the captives. The thought gave her comfort.

A man and a woman came out of what she guessed to be a bunkhouse. The woman cocked her head, staring in open curiosity. The man stared, too, but his glare was cold.

"Butcher!" Edith yelled. A huge, hairy dog rounded the corner of the bunkhouse.

The wolflike creature tore across the ground growling like it might be mad.

Edith opened the door. "Get inside. This is where you'll stay until Mr. Wonderful comes to claim us all."

She stepped into the box of a space. There were no windows, but light fingered through several gaps in the wall. So did the wind.

"Take off that dress and be quick about it." Edith

shed her frayed gown and tossed it at Holly Jane. "Hurry up, girl. A body could freeze to death while you take your time."

"No." She would not give up her gown.

"Oh, you'll give it over, Miss High and Mighty. You see that child over yonder? You give me that dress and it won't get a whippin' for feeding your horse a carrot."

"You are not a kind woman." Holly Jane's anger only made the woman smile. Since she believed that Edith would whip the child, she took off her pretty new gown and handed it over.

Edith Travers snorted. "*Kind* doesn't get you anywhere out here. Hand over them petticoats, too. You can keep your drawers."

"Guard," she commanded the dog. "Butcher is half dog, half wolf and three-quarters wild. He might not bite if you keep still."

Edith slammed the door. A bolt slid into place on the outside.

"I reckon we're stuck in here together, Butcher." She shimmied into Edith's stained gown then sat down on the bare floor. She motioned the dog forward. He hesitated. "Poor pup, I don't suppose you're used to a friendly voice."

Butcher cocked his large head and considered her with wary-looking yellow eyes.

"Come on, fellow. We'll need to keep each other warm."

She opened her arms and he lumbered forward.

His fur felt lush under her fingers, warmer than a thick coat.

"That's a good boy. We'll get on fine, won't we?"

The dog lay down beside her and she curled about him the best she could. A vicious wind shook the shed. The constant creaking made her wonder if the rickety shelter would hold up. If it didn't, if it came apart about her head, she would be able to escape, but to where?

Her only hope was to wait here and pray that Colt came for her.

He would realize by now that she was missing… but did he miss her? There was something he had wanted to tell her…and he had kissed her in front of everyone. That had to mean something.

She huddled deeply into the dog's fur, praying that it did mean something.

How long could a civilized woman get by out here?

She couldn't help but wonder what would become of her if Colt didn't come. Would he even imagine that his cousin had taken her? Would he be willing to come back to a place he hated, if he did know?

Just because he wanted to ride the elephant with her didn't mean that he loved her.

Miles of stark, empty land lay between her and those she loved. Loneliness chilled her as much as the cold night air.

She snuggled into Butcher's fur, seeking warmth

and a friend. When she couldn't call back the single tear that rolled down her face, the dog whined and licked her cheek.

Colt lay flat on a hilltop and watched Cyrus hand Holly Jane over to Edith.

"Damn you," he grumbled when he saw Edith lead Holly Jane to the hostage shed.

When, a few moments later, his cousin came out wearing the red wool dress, he wanted to strangle her, blood relation or not.

Colt shifted his weight to ease the pressure of a rock under his belly.

At least Cyrus had managed to get Holly Jane safely here. Worry had gnawed at his insides the full two days he'd been waiting on the hill. The Good Lord only knew what trouble his cousin might have gotten into along the way…and dumped Holly Jane smack in the middle of it. He'd wager ten dollars that the horses he had ridden in on were stolen.

Colt had taken the train most of the way here, and as he figured would happen, he arrived well before Cyrus.

As much as he had wanted to run his cousin down and snatch Holly Jane right there on the spot, there were other things to consider. He needed time to plan.

Last time he was here, all he'd cared about was seeing his father in the ground and taking Grannie and Aunt Tillie away, clean and fast.

With Holly Jane kidnapped, everything had changed. The Broken Brand had to be destroyed. Some folks might say that he was disloyal to his kin, but there were some relatives who didn't deserve loyalty.

He couldn't spend the rest of his life watching over his shoulder to see if someone he loved was going to be abducted.

This time he couldn't simply ride away. While most of the Traverses were a hair shy of bloodthirsty, they were thieves and cheats. Nearly all of them deserved to go to jail. A few didn't. There were the children to be considered and one kidnapped bride, who hadn't wanted to be forced to the altar.

For their sakes, he didn't do what he wanted to do and sneak Holly Jane away as soon as it turned dark.

It was some comfort knowing that the Traverses would take to their beds tonight not realizing that this would be their last night at the Broken Brand. It was a shame that some of them were not at home. He'd like to see every last one of them behind bars.

His family had taken their last hostage and stolen their last horse.

He watched Edith go into the bunkhouse, the red dress a flame against the dusty earth. His cousin was jealous, a bitter woman as different from Holly Jane as a dove was from a snake.

No doubt, Edith believed that putting the dog in the shed would make Holly Jane tremble all night long, terrified and sleepless. Dogs on the Broken Brand were not pets. They had been raised to intimidate.

Edith would be shocked to know that Butcher was probably wrapped around the prisoner keeping her warmer than anyone in the main house was.

Knowing this is what allowed him to shimmy back from the rise of the hill to join Molly and Silver in a nearby cave.

He wished he had a big furry dog to sleep with since he couldn't light a fire. Smoke would give him away. Also, there were several jugs of kerosene on the cave floor. The warmth of a fire would be only a dream tonight.

He was half tempted to sneak into the shed with Holly Jane and spend the night there. But the ranch dogs would bark. The ones he had been friendly with were long gone.

Everything would be ruined if his presence were discovered too soon.

He reckoned he could ride a mile out, spend the night with the marshal and his deputies, but that would put him out of earshot of Holly Jane in case there was trouble in the night.

He didn't expect there to be, at least not as long as Cyrus kept everyone in check. His cousin, for all that he was a criminal, had odd notions about family loyalty. He would protect Holly Jane if he believed that she was to be the wife of the leader of the pack.

Molly whinnied for his attention so he fed her from a bag of oats, then offered some to Silver.

He was glad that he had brought the horses with him. They were his link to home.

"Sorry, you've got to spend the night in the cave again," he said, because that is what Holly Jane would say to the animals. He patted Molly's neck in the way he had seen her do.

Hell and damn, the horse bumped him affectionately in the ribs with her nose.

It made him feel good, not quite so cold and lonely.

The sun went down fast over the rocky, rugged land. One moment it was dusk and the next dark, no pretty lingering in between, like at home.

It hadn't taken an afternoon for him to feel that William's ranch was the single place on earth where he belonged. It had a way of calling to a man, even over all the miles. It was no wonder that Holly Jane was set on buying the place back, even though that was impossible.

Colt pulled up the collar of his duster and stepped outside of the cave. The wind was a beast, damned if he didn't feel its teeth ripping through the canvas.

He sat on a rock at the top of the hill, watching the hostage shed. It wasn't likely that anyone would venture out tonight, but he couldn't be too careful.

Glancing up, he saw the night sky speckled with stars. If he didn't look down, he could imagine he was home.

Holly Jane huddled close to the dog. He was warm, so she didn't mind that he smelled dusty.

It had been daylight for hours but so far no one had stirred in the main house or the bunkhouse.

Hours ago, before dawn, Butcher had growled and another dog had barked briefly. Far in the distance, she heard footsteps. Probably someone visiting the outhouse.

"Looks like they sleep all day. No wonder the place is a ruin."

The dog licked her hand. She patted his wide head, and watched dust motes twirl in the light streaming through the gaps in the wood walls.

When it seemed that the half the morning had passed and she might die of boredom, the shed door burst open to reveal Edith, probably as warm as a simmer in the pretty wool gown.

The woman inhaled a long draw on a cigarette and let it out slowly.

"My brother says you can cook."

The spray of dark curls crossing Edith's forehead ought to make her look softer, but no curling iron could undo the harsh lines of her face or the nastiness of her scowl.

"Don't sit there staring at me, girl. Get to the house and fix our breakfast."

Holly Jane stepped into the sunshine. She wanted to dash about in relief, to stretch her arms and legs. After being shut up in the shed for so many hours it felt like heaven just to breathe the fresh air.

Edith quashed that jubilation by shoving her in

the spine and pointing the burning tip of her cigarette at the house.

Butcher trotted beside her swinging his ropelike tail.

"I'll fix something special for you," she said to him and rubbed his furry neck. It was interesting and rather nice to be able to stroke a dog and not have to lean down to do it.

"You've ruined him," Edith grumbled. "Next thing you know the beast will be romping with the children."

Edith marched Holly Jane up the front steps.

"Something doesn't smell right." Holly Jane stopped to sniff the chemical odor that lingered near the porch.

"This is the Broken Brand—better get used to that."

Evidently, it was true. Stepping into the house, she had to hold her breath. The scent of sweat and dirty clothing was overpowering. Disorder reigned. She doubted that she would be able to bake a bun if the kitchen looked as bad as the rest of the house.

As it turned out, the kitchen was worse. There was a stove and a table, but grime coated both surfaces.

"Fix something." Edith glared at her then went outside.

A young woman sat on a bench nursing an infant while she told a small boy to put down a knife.

Holly Jane rushed forward and plucked it from his chubby hand.

"Thank you, ma'am." The woman nodded her

head. Her face was pale and drawn, framed by strings of lusterless brown hair. Holly Jane figured she was young, although she didn't look it. "You the new bride?"

"That's what Cyrus thinks."

"Don't let them hold on to you, ma'am, or you'll end up like me."

How long, she wondered, would it take for Colt to come, if he intended to?

Already she felt the hopeless depression of the place. Her hair itched. Her fingernails were imbedded with grime. It wouldn't take long to be so broken of spirit that she had no pride of appearance.

If Colt didn't rescue her, she would, somehow, find a way to escape and bring her friend Butcher with her.

Holly Jane sat down on the bench beside the woman. "I'm Holly Jane." She stroked the baby's fat little foot.

"You marrying Colt Wesson is all Cyrus talks about. Are you going to do it?"

"I reckon we'll see." Her heart squeezed. She wanted that more than the world, but did he?

She snatched the little boy as he dashed past then set him on her lap. "Are you hungry, little man?"

Cooking was bound to boost her courage.

"I'll get us something just as soon as the baby is finished eating. Shouldn't be but a few minutes. I'm Hattie, by the way. The baby is Seth... That squirmy bit is Flynn."

"I'll take care of the food." She set Flynn down

and began to look about for what she could make a meal of. "How many need to eat?"

"There's me and Flynn. There's Joe—he's thirteen—and Libby, who's sixteen, then her little sister, Pansey, who's three. If you could see that they eat first…their folks have died or gone to prison. The others don't pay their welfare much mind."

She would need to sift bugs from the flour, but she could make some flapjacks in a hurry.

"Who else lives here, Hattie?"

"There's Cyrus and his sister Edith, but you've met them. There's a cousin named Charlie and he has a wife, Elise. There's one here who's not a Travers, but a criminal just the same. He's out to wed poor Libby. Doesn't much care that she's no more than a child."

Holly Jane got the bugs out of the flour then scooped a fly out of the lard. In normal times, she wouldn't even serve this food to Lulu, but it looked as though this was all there was at hand.

She must have grumbled…or maybe even cursed, because Hattie sighed.

"I know it's not much, but with Cyrus gone to fetch you and the weather so cold, no one wanted to go on a food raid. They figured they'd wait for Colt Wesson and let him do it."

Holly Jane poured fresh milk into the flour and cracked three eggs into it. The Traverses must have stolen a cow and some chickens.

She stirred the batter harder than she needed to. The man she had fallen in love with would never be a thief like them. This band of ruffians would be sorely disappointed in him.

"Hattie, do you like it here? Do you choose to stay?"

"I have no choice. My hus— The man who brought me here, the father of these babies, was killed in a raid not long ago. I'd like to say I'm sorry…but, what I want more than anything is to go home to my folks."

"Would the rest of them stop you from leaving?"

"Maybe not, but they wouldn't help. I can't take my children and just walk away. The ranch is right in the middle of wasteland. That's why the Traverses are partial to it. In all these years the law never bothered to come and oust them out. I've often wished they would."

Hattie was right—there was nothing for miles but barren earth, fit only for lizards and snakes.

The land was confusing, too. She'd watched, coming in with Cyrus, trying to remember the way. All she'd learned is that on her own, she would become lost in an hour.

The back door squeaked on its hinges.

"Morning, Sunshine. Hope I'm in time for breakfast."

Holly Jane spun about.

Relief and joy flashed in her eyes a heartbeat before she threw herself against him. She hugged him so tight that he felt her slender arms tremble.

He cupped her head to his chest and figured he was trembling, too.

Thank the Good Lord that no one in this viper pit had harmed her.

After a long moment with her squeezing and him cradling her back, the trembling eased. She pulled away to gaze up at him.

Thank the Good Lord, again, that Cyrus hadn't been able to dash her sunny spirit.

It shone out of her eyes, the only warmth for miles around.

"Have you come to claim me…and your rightful place?"

In spite of the fact that she had been kidnapped, spent several days being dragged across Texas, Oklahoma and Nebraska, she looked radiant.

Even the drab, filthy clothes she had on failed to dull her luster.

He brushed his knuckles across the blush on her cheek. It remained even after spending a frigid night in the shed.

"I claim you, Holly Jane, but this hellhole isn't our place."

"Take me home." She stood on his boots, lifted up on her toes and kissed him. Her lips made it feel like they were already back in Friendship Springs and this mess taken care of with nobody having gotten hurt.

"We're going, and soon, but there's something I've got to take care of first. I'll need your help."

She stepped down from his boots and nodded her head. "Whatever you want, as long as we leave here together."

That was his aim, to make ashes of this place then take his woman home.

"Get the children away from the buildings, the farther away the better. I aim to burn this place to the ground and I want everyone well away."

"That was you I heard this morning?" Butcher ambled into the kitchen. Hattie held her baby close and cringed against the wall. Holly Jane held out the palm of her hand and the animal that used to be vicious slid his head beneath it. "I knew I smelled kerosene."

Too bad Holly Jane didn't have the same effect on his family as she did on critters. Today's outcome would be a hell of lot more predictable.

"But what will become of us?" Hattie, who had looked ready to give birth last time he was here, held her infant to her heart and looked at him with equal amounts of fear and hope.

Some folks might say he was the devil for betraying kin, and maybe he was, but the Traverses had caused enough trouble for honest folks. He aimed to stop them this morning.

"Come with us if you like." He didn't think this girl had come to the ranch and been happy about it.

"I'll help Miss Holly Jane see that the buildings are clear."

Hattie glanced at the dog. She braved three steps away from the wall then hugged Colt in a breath-stealing embrace, much as Holly Jane had done. He didn't kiss her, though. There was only one woman he was planning on kissing ever again.

"I'll lay low in the kitchen until I see you've got the young'uns safe." He reached over the dog and drew Holly Jane close. He kissed her quickly one more time. "All hell's likely to break out after that. Molly and Silver are in a cave just over the ridge of the hill just in case something goes wrong."

"Don't say 'just in case' to me. I won't hear anything except that were going home."

"I love you, Holly Jane."

"Don't say that, either. It sounds like goodbye."

He didn't intend for it to be, but he was one against many until the marshal and his gang saw the smoke and came riding in. Anything could happen.

Chapter Thirteen

Colt pinched a flapjack off the griddle. Interesting, he thought while he munched it, that it was Holly Jane to have cooked the last meal in this kitchen.

It felt wrong not to bank the fire in the stove, but what did it matter? It was all going to burn anyway, just as soon as innocent folks were clear of danger.

As far as the others went, seeing the inferno would clear them out of the other buildings like rats on the run.

He walked to the front window and peered through the grimy glass, swallowing the rest of the pancake in a gulp. Churning nerves turned it into a great lump of dough in his belly while he watched for Holly Jane and Hattie.

"So, you came, after all." Edith's voice spoke from behind him. She must have come in through the kitchen.

Curse it, her presence in the house was a complication he didn't have time to deal with. Couldn't very well set the flame with her inside, though.

"You didn't expect me to?"

"I told Cyrus his scheme was harebrained. I never thought you'd come back. I'm surprised it was for a woman. Especially this one—she isn't our kind."

"I wouldn't be here if she was. Take off her dress, Curly Top."

"It's no longer hers." Edith backed into the kitchen, her hands crossed over the bodice of the fine wool.

"That's the trouble with this family." He advanced, she retreated. At the back door he lunged and caught her arm. "You all figure just because you touch something it belongs to you. Take off the damn dress or I'll rip it off you."

"It's cold outside, you'd let your own cousin freeze?"

"Damn straight, I would. Just like you meant to do to Holly Jane."

"I left her my dress."

He couldn't remember a time when he'd wanted to thrash a Travers more than he did right now...even his old man, who had been the worst of them all.

He curled his hands into fists so he wouldn't strike her. "What you gave her was a smelly rag."

"You always were an outsider, blood kin or not."

"The dress, Edith."

She ripped the front open. One button skittered, pinging across the floor.

She glared at him, clearly defying what she considered to be his leadership.

"She won't want you, you know. A fine lady like her and you a Travers."

"There was a time I thought the same, but the last name doesn't make me one of you. It's the fine lady who showed me that."

Stepping out of the gown, she dropped it on the floor. Her underclothes were stained. Sweat marks showed that Edith hadn't bathed in some time.

"No wonder you're a spinster, cousin."

She raked her ragged fingernails at him but he grabbed her arm and hauled her outside. He left the tainted gown where it lay.

"Keep your mouth shut or I'll gag you," he warned.

Edith scowled. He shot the menacing glare back at her and dragged her around to the front porch.

It smelled heavily of the kerosene he had drenched it with before dawn.

He glanced around, relieved to see Hattie carrying her babies, followed closely by Libby toting her sister. Half a minute behind them he spotted Joe and Holly Jane, coming fast, each gripping a frying pan.

"What's going on here?" Edith yanked against his grip.

He let go of her so that he could reach under the porch stair where he had stashed a rag saturated with kerosene.

"I'm taking my leave of this family for good. Say

goodbye to the Broken Brand." He held the rag high and struck a match.

The flame ate the soaked cloth in under three seconds. He tossed it on the porch.

"Better skedaddle." He watched flames gobble the dry wood. Couldn't deny that the sight was satisfying. "Won't be anything left in a minute."

Edith stared at him with her mouth open, seemingly too astounded to move.

"Bunkhouse is next. You might want to sound the alarm."

She spun about and ran, her screech echoing shrilly in her wake.

He ducked into a small building between the bunkhouse and the now fully engulfed main house. This shed held tack and rusty tools. After he had checked to be sure no one was inside, he set the blaze.

The only wood he planned to let stand was the barn. Could be an innocent critter inside that Holly Jane would grieve over.

That thought brought him up short. How had she gotten so deeply inside him that he cared about the fate of chicks and mice?

He shook himself and returned his attention to the task before him.

The building went up in a whoosh. Fire roared and snapped, but that didn't keep him from hearing Edith screeching at the others, calling his name and pointing at the glowing skeleton of the main house.

He figured the marshal and his men had seen the smoke by now and would be on their way.

The lawman had wanted to come in, guns blazing and oust the outlaws on his own terms, but Colt had terms of his own. Because Holly Jane was being held, he'd demanded the time to get her out and the children with her.

For his own satisfaction, he had stood firm on being the one to obliterate the place. He and the marshal had shaken hands on it. Once those two things were accomplished, Marshal Prentis was free to ride in and round up the rest.

The time for purging the Broken Brand was past due; he ought to have done it years ago.

Colt made a quick sweep of the bunkhouse. As he'd figured, everyone had fled to the main house to watch it crumble.

In a minute they'd run back this way, but by then he'd be setting fire to the hostage shed. That one would give him the most satisfaction.

Sparks spit from the body of flames looking like riled hornets searching for something fresh to incinerate. Some went straight up, arching and angry at finding nothing; others shot sideways, and the folks standing too close had to swat at embers in their clothing.

Holly Jane had never seen a structure burn. Back in Friendship Springs, the barbershop had caught fire, but it had happened in the night and she had been a child tucked safely in her bed.

Even from this distance the blaze had a voice. It roared and snapped. It flared suddenly and twisted into the sky with a whir.

"I've never seen anything like that," Hattie gasped while her infant fussed. "I declare, the smoke is black as pitch."

The only building spared from the flames was the barn.

A figure dashed toward them, running through the smoke.

Relief washed through her when it turned out to be Colt, smelling of soot and breathing hard.

He wrapped her up in a hug and squeezed.

"Get everyone to the top of the hill. The marshal and his boys will be here soon, and Cyrus won't like it."

"I won't go without you."

"Damn it, Holly Jane." He kissed her cheek, and she felt the circle of ash it left behind. "I'm counting on you to get the children to safety."

"Let Hattie do it. I'll help you."

He grasped her by the shoulders and stared down hard at her.

"You can't help me. The Traverses came out of the bunkhouse armed. The marshal and his men will come in shooting. Get those people up the hill. I'll be along."

"But you don't have a gun!"

"Don't need one." He kissed her other cheek then dashed away, disappearing in a roll of smoke billowing over the ground.

"Come on." Hattie tugged on her arm. "From what I've heard Colt's better with his knife than most men are with six bullets."

Somehow, that didn't give Holly Jane the comfort that Hattie had intended. If each of the Traverses had six bullets and every one of them was aimed at Colt, it didn't matter how stupendous he was with that long knife.

Since there was nothing she could do for him below, she hurried after the children.

Hattie led the way up the hill while Holly Jane guarded the rear. It wasn't likely that anyone was paying attention to their escape. So much drama was going on below that they wouldn't be missed.

"Just the same," she said to Butcher, patting his shoulder while she walked and craning her neck to see what was going on near the corral. "It's a relief to have you here.... Good dog."

It didn't take long for the buildings to burn. With the noise of the flames becoming quieter, she could make out the voices below more clearly.

She stopped while the others climbed higher. With the smoke less intense, she was able to see figures moving below.

"You're a low-down, snake in the pants traitor, Colt Wesson." Cyrus's voice carried up the hill, louder than the others. "Who gave you the say-so to come riding in here and destroy our ranch?"

"You did. When you kidnapped Holly Jane."

"That was so's you'd take your proper place with a properly taken bride."

"There's nothing proper about this place or any of you."

"That's the point, ain't it?" Cyrus pounded his fists at a puff of smoke drifting past, his agitation clear from halfway up the hill. "Livin' as we please, taking as we please? It was a fine life until you burned it all to cinders."

"You all but sent me an engraved invitation, Mutton Head."

"May Pappy Travers' ghost haunt you for the rest of your life," Cyrus cursed.

"What rest of his life?" Edith shouted. "Shoot him! That's what Pappy Travers would want you to do."

Holly Jane gasped. She locked her knees and clenched her fists to keep panic from laying her flat.

Maybe she couldn't help…but maybe she could.

She had to try. How would she ever take another breath if she remained safely on the hill watching while Colt was murdered by his own family.

She glanced up the hill. Hattie and the children were nearly at the top.

When she spun about to run back down the hill, she slammed square into the chest of a short but stout man.

He clamped his wide, blunt fingers around her throat.

"Where do you think you're getting to, little lady?" His voice sounded like sand, coarse and dry. His slit-shaped eyes stared at her, cool as a reptile's.

From higher up the hill, she heard young Joe shout her name.

The man gripping her shook his head, whistling low. "Someone's going to pay for this mess. I reckon it ought to be you."

Voices filtered up the hill, as clear as if the speakers stood a foot away.

Even if Colt were within reaching distance, she wouldn't call out for help. With bullets threatening, the last thing he needed to do was worry about her.

"What about blood obligation, Cyrus?" She heard Colt say, calm as could be. "Pappy set store in being loyal to blood."

She scratched at the fingers holding her, trying to pry them off.

"Kindly remove your hands from me." She used the same tone on her assailant as she would use on a stubborn suitor and prayed that he didn't detect the quaking under his fingers.

The wide fellow growled and bared his teeth. He didn't notice that the sound caught Butcher's attention.

"Been sick to death of hearing Cyrus talk like paradise was going to come to earth once he brought you here and Colt started leading the raids."

"It seems you don't hold with blood obligation the way Cyrus does."

"I ain't no Travers, don't feel no obligation whatsoever." The pressure around her neck tightened. Dark stars winked in the corner of her vision. "With you and him out of the way, I'll have me a ranch... I'll make Travers, or whatever I decide to call them, a name to be feared far and wide."

Without a rumble of warning, Butcher leaped upon the man, knocked him to the ground and dragged him from Holly Jane.

Loss of air had weakened her and she dipped to her knees, watching while the fat man reached for the gun in his holster.

The dog moved fast. He chomped down on her attacker's arm above the elbow. Blood spurt, a red fountain darkening the dirt. The man cried out, twisting, trying to break free of the teeth ripping into his arm.

After a moment he went still, his flesh as pale as death.

Holly Jane crawled over to him. She plucked the gun from his holster.

"Good boy, Butcher...good dog." He wagged his tail, looking docile even with blood dripping from the fur on his chin.

Joe stood over her, breathing hard from the run down the hill. She handed the weapon to him.

"That's Pete. Hope he's dead," Joe said. "He can't force Libby to marry him if he's dead."

She touched Pete's neck, feeling for a pulse.

"He isn't dead." The cold sweat of his skin slicked her hand. She wiped it on Edith's skirt. "The marshal will be here soon to deal with him. Can you watch, keep the gun handy, in case he comes to before that?"

"Yes, ma'am." The boy squatted beside the outlaw, staring at his face, no doubt watching for a flicker of consciousness so that he could ready the weapon.

"Stay here, Butcher." She stroked his neck. "Good boy."

She stood up then hurried down the hill. It was only a few seconds before she heard the pad of canine footsteps behind her.

The standoff didn't shift while she scrambled down, but tension charged the scene, drawing its stringy fingers around Colt and the outlaws facing him.

Cyrus flexed his hand in an imitation of drawing his gun. The resentment in his expression looked lethal.

Flanking Cyrus on the left, Edith stood in her underclothes looking as though she would happily rip Colt to shreds with her nasty, ragged fingernails.

To the right of Cyrus, was a man, probably the other cousin. His suspenders drooped over his portly belly. He gripped a gun in his fist.

Beside him stood a woman who resembled a slattern more than a wife. She clapped her hands. A twist in her smile indicated that she was enjoying every moment of this showdown and hoping for a bloody end.

Praise Glory that because of Butcher, there was one less villain to face. She glanced up the hill. Joe stood with his knees locked, holding the gun in both hands. Even though he was only a child, she thought he would shoot to protect the others on the hill.

Mercy, she could use that weapon. It couldn't be so difficult to use, just point at something and pull the trigger.

She glanced between Colt, with his knife still sheathed, and Joe, three minutes up the hill. The gun might as well be a hundred miles away for all the help it would be.

"What are you waiting for, Cyrus?" Edith screeched, a foot from her brother's ear. "Shoot him."

"You keep out of man's business," Cyrus snarled at his sister.

"Maybe I would if you'd begin it."

Cyrus punched Edith hard with his elbow. She fell on the dirt, striking her head with a nasty thump. Her foot turned beneath her weight, tweaking it at an unnatural angle.

Holly Jane stared at Colt's back. Terror stole her breath. Any second now a deadly crimson splotch might bloom between his shoulders.

Colt faced two men who had guns and possibly

twelve shots between them. He had one throw of his blade.

There wasn't a blessed thing she could do to help him other than hold on to the dog and remain as still as the stone under her boot. The smallest distraction could cause his death.

"There's things need to be said," Cyrus announced, then glanced sideways at his portly cousin. He nodded at the man's weapon. "Then we can shoot."

The cousin didn't holster his gun, but he did lower it.

"Never took you for a killer, Cyrus." Colt scratched his ear, casually placing his hand within reaching distance of the Arkansas Toothpick. "You held my pappy up as leader, followed him like a devoted puppy on all his crimes, but the one thing the old man wasn't, was a killer."

"Don't you call on Pappy Travers' memory." Cold sunshine sparkled on the sweat beginning to dampen Cyrus's forehead…and, Holly Jane hoped, his gun hand "I was wrong when I thought you could take his place. You've been trouble since your ma died giving you birth. Can't remember when you weren't a cuss and a rotter."

"Can't recall when you were any better." While he spoke, Colt circled slowly west, making both men pivot toward him.

"Where you going?" the other cousin yelled.

"Just getting a better view of your house in ashes, Jelly Belly."

She could see Colt in profile now. He was grinning, trying, she was certain, to stir the hornet's nest.

Any slim hope of a peaceful exit from the ranch was gone. Very clearly, from the burning of the buildings to taunting his cousins, Colt did not intend to let the Traverses continue as they had. If the price was his life, that's what he seemed willing to pay.

She was not.

It wouldn't be much, but she moved her foot, slowly stooped and picked up the stone. Beside her, she felt a tremor shimmy through Butcher's shoulders.

The ground rumbled faintly. She prayed that it was the rumble of horses' hooves and the arrival of the marshal and his deputies.

"Since you're so partial to fire, I reckon you'll enjoy hell," Jelly Belly said, and raised his gun.

Cyrus began to do the same, but he hesitated. Clearly, there was a battle within him. It twisted his expression so that he looked lethal and pitiful all at once. He wanted to kill Colt because he had ruined the family. He shouldn't because of blood obligation. Kin was kin, no matter what. His thoughts were so obvious they might have been written on a page…in blood.

"He's no kin of ours, not anymore," Edith moaned, sitting on the ground and holding her head in her hands. "You do it, Gordie, since Cyrus is too weak."

Cyrus jerked his six-shooter up; it wavered in his grip.

"You shouldn't have forced me to it, Colt." Cyrus shook his head, sorry-like. "I know my duty."

Holly Jane pitched her rock, throwing her whole heart into the effort.

It landed several feet from anyone, but it startled Cyrus and he backed into Gordie.

The hiss of steel cut air. Holly Jane watched a flash of sunlight glitter off the blade of the Tooth-pick as it sliced toward its targets.

Cyrus yelped, dropped his gun and clutched his wrist where blood streamed from a mean gash.

Behind him, Gordie dropped to one knee, Colt's blade imbedded in the flesh of his forearm. The gun dangled from his index finger.

Colt dashed forward, but Edith crawled toward Cyrus faster. She snatched his gun from the dirt then pointed it at Colt.

Gordie shifted his weapon to his good hand. Holly Jane ran at him, a scream trapped in her throat.

A four-legged lightning bolt blazed past her. Butcher charged, placing himself between Edith and Colt.

Edith's gunshot echoed over the smoldering land.

Gordie lifted his gun, his face grimacing with the pain of having the toothpick imbedded in his arm.

Fully focused on his effort, he didn't notice Holly

Jane. She kicked his wrist. A bullet exploded against the ground sending up a spray of grit.

Somehow, in spite of the blow, he kept hold of the weapon. He pointed it at her.

She dropped to her knees, reaching for the hot barrel of the gun, a prayer her only hope that she could knock it away faster than Gordie could pull the trigger again.

Colt's boot slammed his cousin's hand onto the earth.

He snatched up Gordie's gun. In the same movement he plucked the blade from his arm. The man screamed. He passed out.

"Didn't know you were such a scrapper, Sunshine." Colt reached his hand down to her.

She grabbed his fingers. His smile was her lifeline. He wouldn't be grinning if someone had died. She glanced about.

There was a good bit of weeping and moaning.

Cyrus was the loudest. His wrist had a gash that might have killed him had it been deeper. To add to his misery, his sister had shot him in the thigh when Butcher bit her hand and redirected her aim.

Edith had an egg growing on the back of her head and a swelling ankle to go with it. Somehow, Butcher had managed to disarm her without breaking her skin. The blood on her arm belonged to the fellow on the hill.

Gordie, sprawled in the dirt, lay quiet and unconscious. The slattern screeched in a long fit of hysterics with her skirt flung over her head.

She proclaimed at the top of her lungs that Colt was a demon escaped from hell.

As far as Holly Jane was concerned there were angels present.

Not a soul had been killed, and everyone who deserved to be wounded had been.

The rumble of a half-dozen horses' hooves pounded the earth. A few seconds later, Marshal Prentis and his deputies rounded the base of the hill, nearly obscured by the cloud of dust they kicked up.

"You tried to kill me," Cyrus wailed, writhing in the dirt like the snake he'd been since he'd learned to slither.

Colt felt the reassuring warmth of Holly Jane under his arm and tugged her closer. She and the children hadn't been hurt in the ruckus, and that's all that mattered to him.

The others deserved more than what they ended up with. He was relieved that the law was here to give it to them. Too bad some of the Traverses had been away. Still, with the lives they led, it couldn't be long until they ended up in prison, anyway.

"Since you didn't do any lasting harm to Holly Jane, I decided not to."

"Spoiled little princess," Edith grumbled, rubbing her ankle. "So cursed sweet looking. Wish I'd taken my fist to her face."

"See those riders coming in, Curly? That's Marshal Prentis and his men. You're going to have a lot of time to repent of being the truly wicked woman you are."

Holly Jane glanced down at Edith, who glared spitefully at her.

She shrugged, clearly dismissing his cousin and her nasty mouth. "I'm taking Butcher over to the trough to clean him up. He's been quite the hero today."

"He's a beast and going to turn on you!" Edith shouted after Holly Jane.

Colt doubted that. The animal seemed as besotted with his new mistress as every other animal he'd ever seen cross her path. Holly Jane was a special woman, even the beasts recognized it.

"See if he doesn't." Edith shifted her glare to him. "Unlike you, the mutt will be loyal to family once he comes to his senses."

Colt crouched down beside her. His cousin had always been of a hateful temperament growing up. Time had only made her worse.

"Here's a thought to take with you to jail, coz. The one-and-only reason you're sitting here, still breathing, is because of family loyalty."

"Now you sound like a Travers, but the truth is you don't have it in you to kill anyone—you never did."

"I reckon that's right. But I'm sure as hell going

to have a good time thinking of you with no one to harass but the bars on your prison cell."

Colt stood up when the hoofbeats stopped in the yard.

"You aren't dead," Marshal Prentis observed, dismounting his winded horse. "Figured you would be."

The marshal weaved about and around the Traverses scattered on the ground, shaking his head.

"Looks like no one is," he pointed out. "We could use a man like you, Travers, if you'd agree to carrying a gun."

Cyrus grunted something that resembled a harsh laugh. "His own pappy carried the shame."

"He whipped the tail off you all." The marshal took off his hat and swiped the dust from his brow. "Count your lucky stars he made us hold back. You'd probably be facing hell instead of prison if he hadn't."

A deputy guffawed. "One and the same."

Watching Holly Jane over at the trough, cleaning Butcher's face and wearing Edith's sweaty clothing, it was hard to find a shred of pity.

The marshal must have followed his gaze.

"She the lady you came to take home?"

He nodded. "Just as soon as everything's in order here."

"Those the children you mentioned, up there on the hill? What do you plan to do about them?"

"They can come with me if that's their choice," Colt answered. "But even though Hattie was a kidnapped bride, she likely got attached to them. She may want to take them with her, back home to her kin."

"If that's the case, I'll see that they all get there safe."

"I'd be obliged."

"The job is yours, even without a sidearm if you want it." The marshal drew his coat tighter about his chest to ward off the cold.

"Appreciate the offer, Marshal Prentis." Colt glanced behind him at the deputies taking charge of the wounded Traverses. "But I've had my fill of outlaws."

Finished washing the dog, Holly Jane walked toward him. Her hair hung limp and dirty about her face and it stank of smoke. For all that, her smile was fresh and bright.

Holly Jane Munroe was, by a mile, the most beautiful woman he had ever seen…with his eyes or with his heart.

The one-and-only thing he wanted was to take her home and raise horses and babies.

He intended to tell her that just as soon as she was warm, clean and rested.

Chapter Fourteen

Holly Jane sat on a bench at the train depot with a tin cup of hot coffee in her palms. She didn't need to drink it right away... The aroma and the circle of warmth under her fingers were heaven enough.

It had taken nearly two days of hard riding to arrive in the town of Beaverton, a place that Colt had insisted upon coming to because of the train.

The time it took to get home would be cut in half traveling by rail, he had explained.

Well, he would know more about that than she would. Until he bought Granddaddy's ranch, the rails had been his life. She had never even heard a train whistle until an hour ago.

She sat by herself, hunched as far into the corner as she could get. Ladies strolled the platform in clean, fashionable clothing. They chatted and laughed. They hugged loved ones hello and goodbye. She tried not to notice the occasional curious glances cast in her direction.

She looked a fright and she knew it. No doubt she smelled worse. No amount of trying to convince Colt that she was not presentable enough to ride the train would sway his decision that they would travel by rail.

Huddled into his coat against the rising wind, she pressed his hat on her head so that it wouldn't blow off and reveal the horrid mess of her hair.

A long swallow of coffee helped to ease the chill, but even with that comfort, frigid air nipped at her ankles and shivered her knees.

When it came right down to it, ragged-looking or not, she would be relieved to be inside the rail-car with its padded seats. Snuggling in, she would watch the land rush by outside, see the stars track across the sky and all the while be warm behind the glass window.

While she waited for Colt to come back, she thought about Hattie.

The young woman was going home for the first time since she had been carried away. She had come from a good and loving family who would welcome her home with relieved tears and hugs, Hattie had told her. Hopefully they would be as welcoming of the children coming with her.

Marshal Prentis was escorting them home, so they would be safe until then.

Holly Jane breathed in the comforting aroma

drifting up from her coffee mug. She sighed out loud. Life was beginning to fall back into place around her.

What a relief to know that the outlaw gang would soon be locked up good and tight in their prison cells. For the entire first day and night on the trail she had feared that they would somehow charge over a hilltop or pop out from behind a bush.

Whenever she looked over her shoulder or chewed her lip in agitation, Colt swept her from Molly's saddle and placed her in front of him on Silver. He reminded her that the prisoners were in the hands of six armed deputies and that they were wounded.

The only place the Traverses were going was to prison, he had reassured her.

He'd held her, hugged her tight to his muscular chest until her nervousness passed, then she went back to her own horse.

Someday she might tell him that she hadn't been frightened as many times as she led him to believe.

More than an hour had passed and another mug of coffee before she spotted Colt walking up the road toward the station.

The setting sun lit him from behind. He carried a package under each arm. The wind lifted his hair away from his face. It fluttered the sleeves of his shirt. He must be cold to the bone since she was wearing his coat and his Stetson.

"The horses and the dog are bedded down in a

boxcar," he said, his smile warming her like no one else's had ever done. "I wired Grannie and Aunt Tillie that we're on our way home."

All at once the train whistle blew.

"Let's get out of the weather." He shifted both packages to one arm then lifted her with a hand under her elbow.

He led her past one crowded passenger car then another, finally stopping in front of the pretty red caboose.

"Here we are, home sweet home, until this time tomorrow, anyway."

He climbed aboard the back platform, opened the door then reached his hand down for her.

"Oh, my word," she gasped, stepping inside.

The caboose was a furnished room. Heat from a small stove warmed her instantly. There was a round table with a bowl of apples on it. A pair of padded chairs sat beside a window. In the corner was a washstand with a pitcher and a bowl. The bowl had steam rising from it.

She might have run to it and dunked her whole face in the water had she not been so distracted by the bed.

The one and only bed.

Colt watched Holly Jane stare at the bed. He wouldn't press her to share it with him, but he sure as hell hoped she would, once he had his say.

He'd thought about it the full two days between

the Broken Brand and here. He'd spun the words in his mind, this way and that. Nothing he came up with was half convincing enough. What could he say to persuade a pure and lovely soul to join fates with a coarse former outlaw?

Holly Jane turned to him, her eyes bright and joyful even being smudged with weariness.

"How on earth?" She pivoted, taking in the furnished caboose.

"I know the conductor, Lamont. This is his place and he owed me a favor."

Paid in full now, Colt noted. He glanced about at polished wood and freshly changed linens. The stove in the corner gave off waves of warmth. Everything was just as he had requested.

In under two hours his friend had turned the space into an inviting retreat.

A suite in a fine hotel wouldn't have been as nice. And this room moved. They would be home two days sooner by riding the caboose.

A knock tapped lightly on the door. Colt opened it to be greeted by a young woman wearing a crisp white apron. She stepped inside carrying a tray of food covered by a napkin.

"Compliments of the New Beaverton Hotel and Mr. Lamont, sir, for you and your wife." She set the food on the table then hurried out.

Even under a layer of dust, he noticed Holly Jane's blush.

"I don't dare sit down," she said, glancing sidelong at the bed. "I'm filthy."

"No more than I am."

"At least you're wearing your own filth." She lifted the skirt away from her knee. "Half of what I've got smeared on my skin belongs to Edith Travers."

Not for long, he thought, and couldn't help grinning. He must look like the devil with his impure thoughts and a week's worth of beard stubble.

The train jolted into motion. The whistle blew.

Holly Jane lost her balance and fell against him. He caught her waist to steady her. Even under the big duster he felt the sweet curve where her waist flared into her hips.

From the window he watched folks slide past, waving goodbye to loved ones.

He was grateful not to be one of them. His loved one was going home with him.

The wheels picked up speed, clinking on the iron tracks.

"You hungry?" he asked close to her ear.

The brim of the Stetson bumped his mouth when she shook her head. "I'm too filthy to eat."

"About time we took care of that."

He took her hand and led her to the chair that sat beside the washbasin. If he got his way he'd never let go of her hand. As far as that thinking went, he'd never quit touching her at all.

Hell, he couldn't touch her body all the time, but

he intended to touch her heart. He'd live there, right inside even when they were apart.

He sat her down, then dragged a chair from the table and settled across from her.

"Toasty as a heat wave in here." He slipped the canvas duster back from her shoulders and she wriggled her arms free.

He removed the Stetson from her head. She shook her hair free of the constraint. Tangles of blond curls tumbled down her chest.

Lamplight showed a smudge of dirt on her nose and a smear of grit on her cheek.

He picked up the bar of sweet-smelling soap that Lamont had left beside the water basin, dropped it in the water then dipped a clean, soft cloth in the bowl.

"You leave any dust back there on the trail, Sunshine?"

He stroked the rag down her nose and across her cheeks, dipped again and drew the fresh-smelling cloth across her forehead and chin. Last of all he touched her lips, dabbing and stroking the way he intended to do with his mouth.

"Only what you left behind." She reached for the cloth. "I can clean myself."

"I reckon you can." He stroked her throat with warm water.

She closed her eyes. Leaning into the gentle rub, she sighed.

"That feels like heaven. I thought for a while that I'd never be clean again."

Her brown eyes blinked open when he took the cloth away to rinse it.

"I'm glad you burned the ranch down. It wasn't a fit place for anyone to live. That night in the shed I thought about you being just a little boy and forced to live there… I cried myself to sleep over it."

"That was a long time ago."

Life was what it was. It all led him to where he was today…to this moment with a woman he shouldn't deserve. But here she was, gazing at him without blame even though it was because of him that she had been kidnapped.

Today the ranch was a heap of cold ashes, most of it probably blown away by now, along with the guilt of who he used to be.

It was Holly Jane as much as the burning that set him free of his past.

Setting the rag aside, he picked up a new hairbrush that Lamont had provided and turned it in his hand. Until he told her what was on his mind he had no right to continue touching her the way he had a mind to.

"Do you remember that I had something that I wanted to talk to you about the night you were to meet me at the carousel?"

"I remember." Her gaze softened, turning tender upon him.

"The old ladies were right. You are my one." He brushed her cheek with his knuckles. "That's what

I meant when I said I'd never ride the elephant with anyone but you."

"Looks like they are going to get their way... Granddaddy, too, if you are asking for my hand."

He shook his head. "Not just your hand... I want your lips to kiss and your breasts to touch, I want to bury myself in you every night. I'm asking for your heart."

Sliding forward on the chair, he cupped her face in his hands. "I love you, Holly Jane."

He kissed her quick and hard, knowing that fire would flash between them...praying that if she had a doubt about him, passion would sway her decision.

"Marry me... Be my wife."

She blinked, her eyes moist. Seconds passed... a full thirty of them. It couldn't take so long for a simple yes.

A gust of wind hit the caboose straight on and rocked it.

"Grannie and Aunt Tillie thought it would take you longer. They said—"

"You going to marry me or not?"

"Yes, Colt." This time she did the kissing. A white-hot flame seared his soul. "I am."

"I promise to be a better husband than I was an outlaw."

"Thank Glory for that. You didn't seem to do your family proud where thievery was concerned."

"I reckon I'll steal something after all."

Edith's gown on Holly Jane's skin was an insult. He'd been itching to get rid of it for two days.

"Sit back, Sunshine."

When she gazed at him with a question in her eyes, he pushed her backward in the chair with a kiss. Now that he was free to do it, he couldn't seem to quit tasting her.

The wooden button at the neckline of the ugly dress fought his effort to pop it open so he ripped the fabric down the front. It gave with a hiss.

Holly Jane stood up so he wriggled it down her hips then tossed it away…somewhere.

He pressed her shoulders down until she plunked back on the chair.

The water in the basin had cooled so he dumped it out the back door of the caboose. Full dark had settled and clouds hung close to the earth. It smelled like rain.

Back inside, he filled the basin with the warm water simmering on the stove.

He settled back in the chair across from her and dipped the cloth in the soapy water. The scent of flowers filled the caboose when he wrung it out.

There was a smear of grime on her shoulder. He drew the cloth across her skin, erasing it and leaving the fresh floral scent behind. Slowly, he stroked down her arm wiping away the Broken Brand and leaving behind sweet pink flesh.

When he finished, he gave the same unhurried treatment to her other arm.

"I'm going to enjoy marriage." She closed her eyes and sighed deeply. He felt her go limp under his fingertips. "I like it when you touch me."

"So do I."

What he was going to enjoy, was demonstrating just how pleasurable their marriage bed would be.

"What do you say we begin enjoying it tonight?" He slipped a lacy strap from her shoulder. It dragged the fabric down, exposing the upper swell of one tempting, fair-skinned breast.

He couldn't see them yet, but he knew her nipples were pink. Every day since the ride on the elephant, he'd pictured them in his mind, how they matched the blush in her cheeks.

"I say yes." She flicked the other strap off her shoulder and the shift sagged, teasing him while it hung a hair above those pretty buds. If he blew on it, it would fall. "But first I need more soap and water."

He grinned, and she touched his face, tracing the shape of his jaw, then his cheek and his mouth.

Water sloshed in the basin when he rinsed the cloth. A sudden gust of rain pelted the windows. The car rocked slightly in the wind while the clack of the wheels on the track carried the train into the storm.

Colt squeezed the rag then drew it across her chest. A drop of water pearled on her skin then dripped around the inner curve of her breast, vanishing under the lacy edge of the shift.

While he swished the cloth in the water, he gave

the shift a tug. It tumbled to her waist. His heart surged into his throat.

He sat for a moment, simply staring at her chest. It was full and lovely, her breasts pink-tipped just like they had been in his lusty fantasies.

Lifting the cloth from the water, he washed her, one smooth ivory globe then the other. He dropped the towel in the water and lathered his hands with soap.

He cupped both of her breasts, one in each palm, rolling and feeling the slick, plump weight slide against his fingers.

While he watched, the blushed tips twisted with little soap bubbles dotting them.

Holly Jane's breath became shallow and quick. She whispered his name.

All of a sudden he wanted to be finished with the bath, to tumble her down onto the bed. He took a deep shuddering breath to make himself slow down.

Things were different now that she was his promised woman, nearly his wife.

The coach would not stop until tomorrow, and Holly Jane was his for a lifetime. Rushing this moment would be a crime.

She hadn't known, couldn't have guessed, how this moment would be. How it would consume her world until the only thing that mattered was the feel of Colt's hands on her, the sound of his ragged breathing less than an arm's stretch away.

Before, on the carousel, the moment had been intense…arousing, but she hadn't belonged to him then.

Tonight she was free to give herself over to him in every way that a woman could. From this night onward their lives were joined, even though the preacher had yet to give their union the proper words.

Colt rinsed her breasts with fresh water…then with his mouth.

She leaned into him, aching under the suckle of lips and the nip of teeth. Just when she thought she might ooze into a puddle of mush, he backed away.

She opened her eyes and saw him standing over her. He lifted her up then slid her damp underclothes down her hips. She stepped out of them and kicked them away.

He knelt in front of her and washed her leg, stroking her outer thigh then her calf, ankle and foot. He did the same to her other leg.

Drat, her skin was nearly spotless but she was not ready to be finished with his tender, cleansing touch.

Still, there were a few spots he had missed. He stood up and turned her around then washed her back with soapy hands. She gripped the back of the chair, squeezing when he slid his hands around the front and rubbed her belly.

His hands dipped low, circling toward her most feminine spot. She began to tremble. He let go of her, but only for a second. Beginning at her knees he stroked upward, once again circling toward the most intimate place. She could hardly breathe; she wanted him to touch her there that badly.

With her eyes closed she heard him stir the water in the basin. Finally, he stroked her with the cloth, its coarse surface circling waves of pleasure on her sensitive flesh.

Increasingly intense waves of need washed through her. She gripped the back of the chair, holding on to the only solid thing in a dissolving world.

Colt scooped her up. "Are you happy, Holly Jane? Do I please you?"

His bride-to-be smelled like springtime smack in the middle of a fall storm. Sleet smeared the caboose windows and wind howled over and under the moving car.

"You please me, Colt."

Relief eased the band that had cramped his heart. In the past, a woman's approval was something that he had taken for granted. He knew the moves and performed them, a dance that resulted in shallow pleasure every time.

Touching Holly Jane meant something. She was his to love and protect. What she thought of him meant more than anything ever had.

He carried her to the bed and set her on a puffy down quilt. She sank into it, looking like a flesh-and-blood angel reclining on a white cloud.

"Hope you don't mind a man who smells like

a bouquet," he said, glancing back at her over his shoulder while he crossed to the basin.

He stripped off his clothes in a hurry. He didn't want to take the time to wash, not when she was impatient and ready for him, but he did stink. Better to smell like a blossom than a cow pie.

Holly Jane knelt on the bed, watching him.

"Let me wash you," she murmured. "It's a fair turnaround."

He shook his head, scrubbing brisk and fast. He was so hard, so ready, that if she touched him the way he had done to her, he would never make it.

Something ought to be said at a moment as big as this one, but he walked toward the bed with his mouth as dry as a thistle and his head empty of pretty words.

Kneeling on the bed with her shapely bare legs tucked under her, she was more beautiful than a dream. That's what he'd like to tell her. Couldn't, though. When she lifted her arms to him, her breasts jiggled with the movement of the caboose.

The wonder was that he didn't leap upon her like a wild man. No woman had ever made him feel like a savage.

It was a good feeling, but one to be controlled… for the moment, at least.

The mattress sank under the weight of his knees. He crawled to the middle of the bed to where his woman knelt, reaching for him. He pulled her close and wrapped his arms around the smooth skin of her back. The calluses on his hands seemed all the rougher when he slid them over her silky bottom and squeezed.

A purr murmured from her throat. He pressed his mouth against the spot and feasted on the patter of her pulse against his tongue.

He answered her with the growl that he had been holding back. A shiver raced over her skin; he felt the quiver of it under his fingertips.

Bosom to chest, her heat pressed against him. He began to sweat where the plush circles of her breasts slid against him. He burned up when she nuzzled her hips against his shaft.

Easy and slow, he chanted in his mind, *slow and easy.*

All of a sudden Holly Jane yanked his shoulders and tumbled him down on top of her. The bedsprings bounced with a creak and twang.

"Don't treat me like a virgin, Colt." Her breath feathered his lips. "Treat me like a woman."

"You are a virgin?" He wouldn't judge her if she weren't, but hell and damn, he didn't want to share her with anyone past or future.

"Of course, but I'm your virgin." She touched his hair then trailed her hand to stroke his cheek then his lips. "I want the real you to make love to me, not a restrained version of you."

"You asked for it, Sunshine."

With a gentle nip to her belly, he proceeded to taste, pet, fondle and nibble every line and curve of her flesh. He suckled her throat, her breasts and her steamy hot crease.

When he knew she was past ready, he drove into her hard and fast because that is what she demanded of him. She wrapped her legs about his hips, drawing him deeper. She clutched his buttocks in her hands and urged his pace to be fast and hard.

When she shattered, convulsing around him, he arched into her and gave himself up.

He lay on top of her, his limbs tangled in hers, listening to her winded breathing while trying to catch his own.

For a moment he wondered who had been the virgin. Sex had never been so all-consuming.

It didn't take much thinking to know why. The old ladies had been right from the very first day. Holly Jane was his one, from this day forward. No words before a preacher could make their union more blessed.

Which didn't mean that the preacher's blessing was not important. He intended to give Holly Jane the vows just as soon as they collected Grannie and Aunt Tillie from the hotel.

Chapter Fifteen

There was more to Colt Wesson than hard, driving love. During the wee hours of the morning there had been slow, sweet times when he stroked in and out of her as gently as a lapping tide.

Once, he had taken an hour to woo her with languorous kisses and slow simmering petting over every inch of her body. In the end it had turned explosive and left her drained and tingling.

She snuggled against his big bold side, listening to the rain pour down on the coach roof. Half dozing, she watched the drops race across the glass in a smear. Dawn couldn't be far off. The clouds were beginning to lighten.

"You awake, Sunshine?" Colt stroked her head then twined his fingers through the length of her hair.

"More or less," she admitted with a yawn.

"You aren't marrying me for the ranch, are you?"

She eased up onto her elbow and gazed down into his face. The shadow of a frown line crossed his brow.

"No, Colt." She smoothed the lines with her fingertips. "You aren't marrying me so I can't take it back, are you?"

"You found me out."

She laughed and tickled his face with the ends of her hair. "The second time I saw you, when you were still a stranger leaning over my bed, I suspected you could be my one."

"Grannie said something of the same to me the day before. I reckon when Aunt Tillie agreed, I ought to have paid them more mind."

"Well, it took the pair of us a mite longer to sort through the doubts, but here we are."

"The minute we get home," He stroked his hand over the curve of her hip. "What do you say we pick up Grannie and Aunt Tillie and head straight for the preacher? I'm done with cold nights in the barn."

"The sooner we produce little Emily, the happier they will be."

"Not just them, Holly Jane—me, too." He tickled his fingers over her belly. "Ponies aren't the only thing I want galloping over our ranch."

He flipped her over and rolled on top of her. Hard, lean muscles pressed her into the mattress. "All this activity has worked up my appetite. The train makes a stop in an hour or so—what do you say we get off and hunt up some breakfast?"

"I say I'll never get dressed again if it means putting on Edith's dress."

"Never?" He tickled her ribs then stopped to kiss each of her breasts when they jiggled with her laughter.

With a wink he eased off her then got out of bed.

He went to the small table beside the window and picked up the pair of packages he had left there.

The train whistle blew. That must mean they were passing a town. She had learned that much about rail travel during the night.

"Wait!" She raised her hand, palm forward.

"What? A mouse run across the floor, Sunshine?"

"No, I want to look at you is all."

That dimpled grin would intrigue her for the rest of her life. He turned his naked body this way and that. Muscles shifted under skin kissed golden by the flickering lamplight.

She was hungry...very hungry. She wouldn't even have to put on a stitch to appease her appetite.

Colt plopped his handsome body down on the bed.

"Here's something to keep you decent."

She reached for the largest of the paper-wrapped packages.

"This first." He handed her the smaller one.

She ripped the paper and a froth of lace undergarments fell out. An ivory-colored shift came open in her lap. Glittering up from the folds was a delicate gold band engraved with an etching of the sun and a small ruby at the heart of it.

He picked it up and slid it on her finger. It winked and sparkled.

"No going back now, Sunshine. You're mine, good and claimed."

"It's so beautiful!" She held it to the lamplight to watch it shine. "How on earth?"

"While Lamont ran around taking care of everything else, I went shopping."

"I could go my whole life wearing just this." She pressed the gold close to her heart. "But think of the scandal it would cause. Friendship Springs might never recover."

"I reckon you should open the other package."

In that one there was a yellow skirt and a blouse that looked like a spring bouquet...also a coat that would be warm and snug.

She planted a kiss on his mouth then scrambled off the bed.

"I can't get used to kissing you whenever I feel like it." It gave her the most wonderful sense of belonging.

Gathering up Edith's rag from the corner where Colt had tossed it, she marched to the stove, opened the door and shoved it in.

"There goes the last of the Broken Brand," he said, grinning.

"I love you, Colt." She adored her brand-new intended so completely that she was about to burst with the joy of it. How odd that a tear stung her eye. She dashed it away with the back of her hand.

The breakfast stop wouldn't be for an hour or more. She launched herself at the bed right into Colt's open arms.

It was good to be home. Holly Jane rode into town on Molly's back feeling the peace, the tranquillity of being in the place she loved.

Riding beside her on Silver, Colt leaned over and whispered something inappropriate and delightful in her ear.

"What do you say, Sunshine? Let's wait to pick up Grannie and Aunt Tillie from the hotel until the morning…give ourselves one more night."

"That would be wonderful." She wanted nothing more than to urge Molly to gallop all the way to the ranch then race Colt up the stairs and into the bedroom. "And very selfish."

"I reckon you're right. They'll be worried about you."

"No more than they are about you."

Holly Jane sat tall in Molly's saddle, glancing at the homes along Main Street. Butcher trotted in front of the horses, wagging his big hairy tail.

The dog didn't appear to miss his old home. He bounded along like nothing was wrong.

"Something is wrong." She turned to stare at Colt, the first fingers of apprehension knotting her belly. "Where is everyone?"

Typically, the hour before sunset found neighbors on porches, visiting and chatting over their day. They might bundle up because it was November, but in Friendship Springs, visiting was an evening ritual.

"It's clear as a bell outside, so why do you suppose the storm shutters are closed on every house?" she asked.

"Stay close." Colt clicked his tongue. Silver picked up his pace.

Every shop in Town Square was shuttered and closed. Reining the horses in front of the hotel, Colt slid from Silver's saddle.

There was a note tacked to the front door. He took the steps up two at a time. After he read it he turned toward her, his face grim.

"Closed for business." He mounted Silver. "We'd best get home."

It didn't take long. The horses pounded the wooded trail like a bag of golden oats waited for them at the end.

"Grannie!" he bellowed, crossing the bridge. "Aunt Tillie!"

He leaped from the saddle and let the horse find its way to the corral while he ran up the stairs.

The front door opened before he reached it. Lamplight spilled into the dusk.

The old ladies stepped out and Colt wrapped them up in a great hug, Grannie Rose in one arm and Aunt Tillie in the other.

"You two all right?" He kissed one wrinkled cheek then the other. "What's going on in town?"

Holly Jane dismounted Molly, who followed Silver to the corral.

"The Broadhowers think that the Folsoms kidnapped Holly Jane. And the Folsoms think that the Broadhowers did it." Aunt Tillie broke from Colt's embrace to hug Holly Jane. "Of course, we knew better. We are so glad that you are both home safe and sound."

"Is that our Butcher, or just a vision, off to join the others in the garden?" Grannie Rose ruffled the fur on the dog's thick neck. "He seems real enough to me."

"It's him, Grannie, fleas and all," Colt assured her.

"He'll be a help, then, when the war starts."

Cold dread tightened Colt's gut. One of two things was happening and neither one of them were good. Either there was about to be some sort of conflict with Holly Jane at the heart of it, or Grannie's mind was failing fast.

"Aunt Tillie?" he asked, bracing for bad news.

"Let's go inside," she said. "It's turning colder by the minute."

"I'll see to the horses."

"Don't dillydally," Aunt Tillie ordered. "That ring on Holly Jane's finger says we've got some catching up to do."

"I hope we haven't missed anything," he heard Grannie say.

"We wouldn't do anything without you and Aunt Tillie," Holly Jane answered.

The truth was that they had done everything short of the vows. And that's something he intended to take care of in the morning.

Hell and damn if he was going to let the Folsoms and the Broadhowers use Holly Jane as an excuse to destroy each other.

Fifteen minutes later, with the horses and the dog settled, he walked back to the house. The boy that he had hired to take care of the animals while he was gone had done a fine job. He would be sure to give him an extra dollar.

Coming in the back door, he went through the kitchen then into the parlor. He found his intended seated between Grannie and Aunt Tillie in front of the fireplace. The pig sat on her lap snuffling down a cookie. His heart warmed and it wasn't due to the heat of the flames in the hearth.

Only Holly Jane could coddle a side of bacon. He hoped the critter stayed small. Chances were slim that it would ever spend a night in the barn with the rest of the livestock.

It would only be a matter of time before she brought Butcher inside.

He considered that for a moment while he gazed at the three women in his care. The hound would be better able to protect them if he was in the house.

Later on tonight, when he made a final check on the animals, he'd brush the dirt out of the dog's fur and bring him inside.

"Well—" Grannie pointed to the vacant chair before the fire "—tell us everything. Did you kill your cousin?"

"I felt like doing it," he admitted, sitting in the chair beside Holly Jane and stretching his boots toward the warmth. "Didn't need to, though, since he didn't do Holly Jane any lasting harm."

"Your grandson did a thorough job of burning down the ranch, though. And everyone who needed to go to jail, did."

"What about poor little Hattie…and the children?" Auntie Tillie asked, leaning forward in her chair, concern etched in the lines about her eyes. "What became of them? It was near Hattie's time when we left."

"The baby, Seth, has a lusty set of lungs for such a tiny thing. The marshal took the lot of them home to Hattie's folks."

"That is good news. The sweet girl never did take to being a Travers. She was like you in that way, Colt," Grannie said.

"And speaking of good news—" he nodded his head at his intended then reached for her hand "—you noticed the ring on Holly Jane's finger?"

"We thought you'd never come in from the barn and tell us about it." Aunt Tillie clapped her delicately veined hands then folded them in her lap.

"We were about to burst," Grannie said.

"Turns out the two of you were right. Holly Jane is my one. We're getting hitched as soon as I can clear it with the preacher."

Aunt Tillie hugged Holly Jane then hurried to the kitchen and returned a moment later with a bottle of wine and four glasses.

Given a choice, he'd live in this moment forever, with the three women he loved gathered around the fireplace, laughing and toasting Emily and Alexander.

But he hadn't been given a choice. The feud was coming to a head, like a boil ready to burst, and his bride-to-be was at the center of the ugly mess.

A day had passed since Colt brought her home. Holly Jane paced across the front porch, watching him gallop away on Silver.

This was the third time he had gone to town since then. Each time he came home he reported that tensions were tightening. The only folks on the streets were the ones who had to be…and a few stray dogs.

Children stayed home from school. The saloon was boarded up. Someone had moved past the window inside the hotel, he'd told them, but the Closed sign remained on the door.

Those who did venture out moved quickly from one building to another, glancing worriedly over their shoulders.

This was not what Granddaddy had intended for

his town. From the beginning it was to be a place of harmony among neighbors, and mostly it was... except when it came to the Folsoms and the Broadhowers.

Holly Jane shivered in the cold. She spun about then and went back inside the house to bake another batch of chocolate cookies. This kept Grannie happy, but didn't do a thing to soothe her own nerves the way it usually did.

What, she wondered, was Colt doing now? Yesterday morning, he had gone to speak to the preacher and arrange their wedding.

The sooner the better, when it came to that. It was not easy falling asleep knowing that her man was in the room across the hall, maybe naked, maybe— well, she couldn't dwell on that right now.

Had it not been for Grannie and Aunt Tillie, she would have spent the night where her heart belonged...where all of her would belong, the day after tomorrow.

Maybe as soon as she was married, things in town would cool off. If they had no hope of controlling the carousel land, perhaps the Folsoms and the Broadhowers would give up.

It wasn't likely, since their hatred of each other went beyond her part in it. Still, what if she promised not to dam up the water to either family?

But no, hadn't Granddaddy promised the same?

Colt believed that the feud had gone too far for anyone to listen to reason.

"Don't you worry, dear. Our boy can take care of himself. He grew up having to, what with his pappy being worse than no pappy at all." Aunt Tillie stood at the front door watching Colt disappear into the woods.

"I know he can, in a face-to-face fight. I saw that at the Broken Brand. But, Aunt Tillie, Colt is all that's standing in the way of either of those families taking this ranch, and neither of them favors a fair fight."

"He knows that. He'll be careful…and not only because he loves this place, but because he loves you. Our Colt won't be careless and leave you unprotected."

Not on purpose. But she wouldn't put it beyond his enemies to shoot him in the back. The picture in her mind made her want to retch.

Grannie pushed Lulu off her lap, joined Tillie at the door and gave Holly Jane a hug around the middle.

"Won't you fix us up a pot of hot chocolate, dear? It will make us all feel better."

Midday had come and gone. Where was Colt?

Even Aunt Tillie and Grannie seemed nervous, which made her want to crawl out of her skin. Those ladies had seen a lot in their lives and were normally as cool as a pair of melons in a summerhouse.

"I'm going for a walk," she told Aunt Tillie.

"I reckon it won't hurt as long as you stay close to the house…like Colt said to."

It wasn't so much that Colt had asked her not to leave the ranch—it was more that he had demanded it. So far only the preacher knew where she was, and that is how he wanted it to stay.

Things were dangerous in town, especially for her. She understood that. By going there she would be placing him in danger as much as herself since he would face any risk to protect her.

With Butcher on one side of her and Lulu on the other, she crossed the bridge. She walked toward the path, pausing now and again to listen for the beat of Silver's hooves on the trail.

The woods were quiet with November's cold weather settling in. If he were coming, she would hear him from far off.

Silence and more silence strained her ears.

There had to be something she could do. She was in the thick of this mess whether she wanted to be or not. If a battle did break out between the families, each believing the other had kidnapped her, people might be hurt…even innocent children.

She ought to show herself. It might defuse things for a time.

That would not solve the issue of them both coveting her land, though.

There was nothing she could do, absolutely nothing…except.

She went suddenly still then bolted toward town

with Butcher bounding on one side of her and Lulu squealing behind.

Running, she prayed that Granddaddy would understand.

Chapter Sixteen

Old man Folsom marched through the woods carrying a rifle. His breath trailed behind him like a cloud in the snapping air. He turned to glance behind him at the two young men following, also carrying firearms.

"Hurry up, you old women! It's past time that those Broadhowers paid for all the years of…"

Colt sat on Silver's back, visible among the trees, but the men didn't appear to notice him.

The old fellow shook his fist at the sky for some reason that Colt couldn't understand. Looks like the boys didn't either because they shook their heads. Still, they trailed after the old man, rifles in hand.

"And now they've kidnapped Miss Munroe!" he roared. "They'll see every one of us in our graves if we don't do something about it right now."

"Maybe they didn't take her," Billy Folsom, a

young man who had been one of Holly Jane's suitors, spoke up.

"She's gone, ain't she?" He shook his fist, this time at a passing cloud. "Who else would have done it?"

"Could be she went someplace of her own free will," the other boy pointed out.

"Don't be a dimwit, Chester."

"He's just saying, Grandpa, those Broadhowers think that we took her."

"Just goes to prove that family is all liars, have been from the very beginning."

"I heard that you and old man Broadhower were friends once." Billy, as young as he was, had to quick foot it to keep up.

"I reckon everyone's danced with the devil a time or two. Least that's one Broadhower gone to hell. This afternoon there's going to be a whole lot more of them."

Billy stopped and set the mouth of his rifle toward the dirt. "What if I don't want to kill anyone?"

"Then you can find yourself a new family, boy. Now get along, we're keeping the others waiting."

Colt watched the trio disappear into the trees.

He'd spent a number of hours watching the woods, making sure that no one approached the ranch.

Holly June was safe at home and he meant to keep her that way. There had been a time when he would have watched over her out of obligation to William, but not now. Now he did it because she was his future.

Out patrolling the woods and keeping an eye on the town, there had been plenty of time for his mind to wander.

Too often, it wandered to a life without Holly Jane. That was a future he wanted no part of. Whatever the hell happened between the Folsoms and the Broadhowers, Holly Jane would be well away from it.

When the voices of the men faded, he turned Silver south, taking the trail through the woods that led to the saloon. He had noticed earlier in the day that the Watering Can had reopened.

Since the marshal hadn't been in his office all day, or at home, Colt hoped to corner him in the saloon. Hell was about to break out in town, and the man had an obligation to take care of it.

A thought hit him. It whooshed the breath right out of his lungs. Could be that making other folks live up to their obligations was a Travers trait. He didn't want to admit that he was like his cousin in any way, but here he was, on his way to confront the lawman and convince him to do his duty.

Coming inside, he was greeted by warmth and quiet conversation. Half a dozen men sat about a table, drinking and discussing the unease that each of them had seen in town while on the way here.

The marshal sat in a corner by himself, smoking a cigar.

"Afternoon, Travers." The blacksmith greeted him with a nod. "Come sit with us."

"Maybe later," he answered to be polite, but with everything going on, he couldn't sit still if his pants were nailed to the chair. "I've come to speak with the marshal."

Six disgusted glances pivoted the lawman's way.

Colt crossed the room. The conversation at the table fell silent.

Colt scraped a chair away from the table, propped his leg on the seat and crossed his arms over his knee. He stared down at the lawman. "Don't you have a town to save, Wyatt Earp?"

"Used to." His voice quavered. It was pitiful. The man responsible for the well-being of the folks in Friendship Springs had a face as pale as watered milk...and his jowls jiggled.

"There's a rumor that Miss Munroe has been kidnapped by the Folsoms. You intend to ignore that?" he asked.

"I heard it was the Broadhowers that did it," said a man at the table.

The marshal seemed to sink in upon himself. He snuffed out his cigar.

"She isn't kidnapped at all," the blacksmith answered. "I saw her go into the mayor's office not half an hour ago, dragging the lawyer with her."

What the hell and damn was the woman doing in town? She'd hear a mouthful from him when—

A gunshot cracked from the north end of town. Another one spit an answer.

A shotgun blast rattled the front window of the mayor's office.

Holly Jane grabbed a document off the front desk, the signatures still damp. Lulu scrambled for cover under the mayor's desk, where she would probably remain for the rest of the week.

Butcher, apparently used to gunfire, didn't hesitate to dash out the front door when she did.

She couldn't be too late…please don't let her be too late to stop the violence.

An answering shot split the quiet afternoon, coming from two blocks north of her.

Folks who had been too cautious to come outside over the past two days, drew aside the curtains over their windows, looking surprised to see her.

She heard a door open, then another and another.

In the street up ahead, she spotted her grandfather's old friend, Hyrum Folsom, the only one of Friendship Springs' founders still alive.

But he wouldn't be for long if he didn't drop the weapon he had pointed at Henry Broadhower.

A hundred feet away, on the opposite side of the road, Henry braced his legs. Because of his injured shoulder, his left arm was in a sling, but in the other hand was a pistol. He was flanked by half a dozen men and boys with weapons of their own.

Hyrum was backed up by his men, Billy amongst them.

Her heart sickened. Billy was a decent young man. If he died in the street in front of her she couldn't bear it.

"Time you all met your evil maker!" Hyrum shouted. And raised his rifle.

"It's Folsom blood that'll be spilling on the street if you don't hand over Holly Jane!" Henry lifted his gun.

She ran as fast as she could with Butcher keeping pace.

"Stop!" she shouted, hoping that she could be heard above all the cussing being fired back and forth.

"Wait!" She stood, barely able to catch her breath, between the angry families.

Everyone grew silent, staring at her. The dog paced a circle about her, growling and looking like his name.

"There's no need for a fight," she gasped. "No one kidnapped me. I was on a trip."

"You walk over here to me, Holly Jane," Henry barked, waving his pistol. "You marry me this afternoon and I won't kill anyone."

"You take a step that way, Miss Munroe, and you'll be the first to fall." At this moment, it was hard to believe that Hyrum Folsom had ever been Granddaddy's friend.

"You don't need me, Henry. You either, Mr. Folsom." She stood still, afraid that a quick movement might cause the men to begin shooting. She heard voices but they seemed distant, muffled…and horse hooves clapping on the road, coming hard and fast.

"Not you." Henry's voice sounded like a growl, and Butcher bunched his shoulders. She touched the dog gently, told him with her fingers not to leap. "Your land, though. I need that to dry out the Folsom maggots for good."

"Shoot that girl, Billy," Hyrum shouted. "Before she hightails it out with Lucifer."

"Do it yourself, if you're going to." Billy tossed his rifle in the dirt. "I reckon I will find me another family."

The sound of the hoofbeats halted all of a sudden, then someone was running but she couldn't look.

Then there was Colt, standing beside her with his big knife drawn.

A dozen firearms swung toward him from both sides of the conflict. With a firm hand on her shoulder, he shoved her down so that she was somewhat sheltered between his legs and Butcher's bulky body.

"You all go on home." He glared at the Folsoms, then the Broadhowers.

"Says you and that piece of tin?" Henry snickered. So did some others.

"It won't get everyone, but it'll get you." Colt balanced the handle in his fingers. "Eyeball or throat? Your choice, Sap Head."

"You can all put down your weapons!" Holly Jane came slowly to her feet so as not to startle anyone into shooting. She waved the document the lawyer had drawn up. "I no longer own any property. I've donated the carousel land to Friendship Springs. It belongs to all of us now. No one can run anyone else dry."

That shut everyone up in a hurry. Colt ripped the paper from her hand and stared at it.

"That's as sweet as one of your chocolate cakes, Miss Holly Jane," Henry said, but he wasn't smiling. "What's to keep me from killing the both of you and taking your grandfather's ranch for myself?"

"There's me to keep you from doing it." Old man Folsom shook his fist. "I'll kill you before you get an inch of William's land."

"And us, Uncle Henry!" Susan Broadhower ran forward to stand between her uncle and Holly Jane. Six other young Broadhowers followed, making a buffer between her, Colt and the guns.

Hyrum laughed, the cackle brittle and demented. "Looks like I win, unless you aim to shoot down your own kin."

"You don't win, either, old man." Billy strode forward with Lettie Coulter on his arm. The pair of them faced the elder Folsom. "We're tired of your feud. We aren't participating anymore."

A rumble of young voices drowned the old man's

cursing. A dozen Folsoms strode from behind a building to stand up to the old man.

Colt sheathed his knife because all of a sudden there were more of them, young folks gathering in the street and mingling, shaking hands and embracing.

Young Folsom mothers cooed over Broadhower babies. Men on both sides lowered their weapons, some to stalk away toward home but more to join the mulling crowd.

The folks of Friendship Springs came out of their homes, bringing their children with them.

Holly Jane glanced about. There had to be near sixty people meeting peacefully.

Billy Folsom stood on top of a box on the board-walk. He offered a hand to Susan Broadhower, bringing her up to stand beside him.

"On behalf of the Folsom clan, I thank Holly Jane for the gift to Friendship Springs." He hesitated for half a second then looked at his grandfather. "I hereby declare this feud over. Here's my handshake on it to Suzie Broadhower."

He put out his hand. Susan shook it up and down.

"I also declare on behalf of the Broadhower clan that the feud is over and done."

Cheers went up in the street. People tossed hats in the sky.

Colt hugged Holly Jane to him. Butcher mingled with the revelers, slapping his tail on skirts and trousers.

Over the cheers, Holly Jane almost missed hearing the gunshot. The blast shook nearby windows. Everyone hit the ground.

When she looked up, Henry Broadhower lay dead on the street. Hyrum Folsom stood over him, shaking his fist at the sky, laughing and clearly insane.

Billy leaped from the bench and approached his grandfather, slow and steady.

"Grandfather, put down the gun," he said quietly, soothingly.

Folsom swung the rife, pointing it at his grandson's chest.

"You ain't got no authority to call off nothin', you worthless whelp. Should have strangled you the day you were born."

"I know you don't mean it, Grandfather. Just set the gun on the ground."

He did mean it. Holly Jane felt it in her bones. Butcher hurried back to her. She felt his low growl under her hand.

Colt dropped his arm from around her back. She felt him rise to his knees, then his weight shift. A second later she watched his blade cut the air, heard the hiss before the blade sliced through Folsom's shirt and imbedded in his shoulder.

Billy caught the rifle and his grandfather before they hit the ground.

Colt stood beside the window on Christmas Eve watching snowflakes fall past the window pretty as a blessing.

He couldn't recall where he'd spent last Christmas. More than likely, he'd had dinner at a hotel then spent the rest of the holiday alone. Or maybe he had worked.

A snowflake swirling light and happy on the breeze hit the window, revealing a delicate pattern before it melted.

Because of William Munroe, blessings fell upon him like the snow in the yard. He lifted his mug of coffee in a silent toast to his late friend. If it weren't for William, he wouldn't be here in his own home with his wife in the kitchen, making the house smell like chocolate, cinnamon, mint and love, all in preparation for the guests stopping by tomorrow.

Blessings had fallen upon Friendship Springs, as well. With the cankerous influence of Hyrum Folsom and Henry Broadhower lifted, the town was becoming the one that William had envisioned.

Holly Jane had been a big influence on the healing of the town by donating her carousel land for a park. The carousel remained her personal property, and she was the caretaker of the park. But the land belonged to everyone. It was open on Sunday afternoons and for special events.

Just last week a wedding had taken place. Billy Folsom had married his Lettie with the whole town present to wish them well.

It wasn't paradise, not quite yet. There were still some hard feelings between the older members of the families, but the young folks were bringing them around. The feud itself had been buried with Henry Broadhower. It had been imprisoned with Hyrum Folsom.

Day by day, Friendship Springs was becoming the place that William had planned for it to be.

Wherever Munroe was in the great hereafter, he was bound to be grinning. He'd been as cunning in his matchmaking as the old ladies had been blatant about it.

Colt inhaled a deep breath of fresh-cut pine. Bringing home the Christmas tree that morning had been something. Holly Jane had been so hopping with pleasure over it that it might have been her first tree.

It was the first tree for him, Grannie and Aunt Tillie. It was hard to recall when he'd seen the ladies so happy…other than a month ago when they had dressed in their finest and stood with him and Holly Jane as they recited their wedding vows.

He couldn't get over how pretty the tree was, with the candles glowing warm on the boughs and garlands of popcorn strung all about

"Well, there you are!" Grannie exclaimed, coming into the parlor with an apple tart in her hand.

She went to the fireplace and bent over the dog and the pig where they slept curled about each other. Aunt Tillie followed behind her, carrying a plate of chocolate cookies

"Here you go, then." Grannie broke off a piece of

pie to feed to the pig then gave the rest to the dog. "Now, you are to leave the cookies for Santa alone."

Aunt Tillie set the cookies on a table next to the fireside chair.

"I can't recall when I've been so happy." Grannie crossed the room and hugged him about the waist. "Do you reckon Santa will really leave me a gift. He never has before."

"He only brings gifts to well-behaved people, Rose," Tillie answered.

"It makes sense then," she sighed. A second later her face creased in a huge smile. "I believe I've managed it this year."

"I reckon you both have." Colt gave each of them a hug and a kiss on the cheek."

"I probably wouldn't have seen Santa in the garden a while ago if he didn't plan on leaving a gift."

"I'm sure that's true, sister. We'd best get up the stairs and into bed."

"Visions of sugarplums," he said quietly, watching them mount the stairs, arm in arm.

Several moments later, Holly Jane peeked her head out from the dining room. A dab of flour dotted her nose and dusted her cheeks.

"Have they gone up?"

How, he wondered, was it possible to love another person as much as he loved her? This time last year he wouldn't have believed it to be true.

His beautiful, happy wife had taken his dreary

life, shaken it to its core, and then handed it back full of sunshine.

From that first day in The Sweet Treat, he had felt her warmth. She was his Sunshine, just like the engraving on her wedding band.

"I reckon Grannie will spend the night watching out the window, waiting for Santa to come back to the garden," he said.

"Well—" she stepped into the room with her arms full of gifts "—I hope he does."

She knelt beside the tree, setting a gift here and a present there, then rearranging them until the look suited her.

He knelt beside her. His gift to her was already under the tree, hidden toward the back so she wouldn't see it. It was the framed deed to their home, her name on top of his.

"You'd better eat one or two of those cookies, Santa," she said, gazing at him with brown sugar eyes that seemed even warmer than usual.

"I reckon I'd rather eat you."

He tipped her chin up then kissed her, long and deep. He came away with the taste of cinnamon on his lips.

"I never figured Christmas would be this much fun."

"Just wait until tomorrow."

"I love you, Holly Jane."

"I love you, too, Colt."

He glanced down at a small package wrapped in red fabric.

"Is that the one?" he asked, brushing his fingers over the green bow.

She nodded her head, her cheeks flushing pink. She covered his hand with hers.

Together, they stared at the package. He figured her smile went clear to her heart, same as his did.

"Do you suppose they'll be surprised?" she asked.

"Not too surprised." He kissed her again, couldn't help it. "I wonder what their prediction will be, the blue booties or the pink ones?"

"What if it's both?"

He couldn't seem to find the words to answer her, to tell her how pleased that would make him so he laid her gently down in front of the Christmas tree to show her.

* * * * *

REQUEST YOUR FREE BOOKS!

 HARLEQUIN® HISTORICAL:
Where love is timeless

2 FREE NOVELS PLUS 2 FREE GIFTS!

YES! Please send me 2 FREE Harlequin® Historical novels and my 2 FREE gifts (gifts are worth about $10). After receiving them, if I don't wish to receive any more books, I can return the shipping statement marked "cancel." If I don't cancel, I will receive 6 brand-new novels every month and be billed just $5.44 per book in the U.S. or $5.74 per book in Canada. That's a savings of at least 16% off the cover price! It's quite a bargain! Shipping and handling is just 50¢ per book in the U.S. and 75¢ per book in Canada.* I understand that accepting the 2 free books and gifts places me under no obligation to buy anything. I can always return a shipment and cancel at any time. Even if I never buy another book, the two free books and gifts are mine to keep forever.

246/349 HDN F4ZY

Name	(PLEASE PRINT)	
Address		Apt. #
City	State/Prov.	Zip/Postal Code

Signature (if under 18, a parent or guardian must sign)

Mail to the Harlequin® Reader Service:
IN U.S.A.: P.O. Box 1867, Buffalo, NY 14240-1867
IN CANADA: P.O. Box 609, Fort Erie, Ontario L2A 5X3

Want to try two free books from another line?
Call 1-800-873-8635 or visit www.ReaderService.com.

* Terms and prices subject to change without notice. Prices do not include applicable taxes. Sales tax applicable in N.Y. Canadian residents will be charged applicable taxes. Offer not valid in Quebec. This offer is limited to one order per household. Not valid for current subscribers to Harlequin Historical books. All orders subject to credit approval. Credit or debit balances in a customer's account(s) may be offset by any other outstanding balance owed by or to the customer. Please allow 4 to 6 weeks for delivery. Offer available while quantities last.

Your Privacy—The Harlequin® Reader Service is committed to protecting your privacy. Our Privacy Policy is available online at www.ReaderService.com or upon request from the Harlequin Reader Service.

We make a portion of our mailing list available to reputable third parties that offer products we believe may interest you. If you prefer that we not exchange your name with third parties, or if you wish to clarify or modify your communication preferences, please visit us at www.ReaderService.com/consumerschoice or write to us at Harlequin Reader Service Preference Service, P.O. Box 9062, Buffalo, NY 14269. Include your complete name and address.

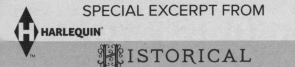
It had been a mistake, asking him to dance. It made it impossible for her to ignore the fact that she was attracted to him. She liked the soft burr of his accent, which made her think of misty Scottish glens and rugged Highland scenery. She liked the combination of auburn hair and grey-blue eyes and the latent strength she could feel in that lean, hard body. She liked the hint of sensuality in his unsmiling mouth. For once, she saw not the soldier but the man.

And she so desperately wanted to be held. Not to think. Just to be held. Sylvie relaxed a little, allowing him to draw her closer. He smelled of expensive soap, unlike most of the soldiers, and also a little of that dank, muddy smell that clung to all of them. But mostly he smelled intoxicatingly male.

She closed her eyes. She forgot she was in the club. She forgot the guilt at being alive that dogged her every waking moment. She forgot everything save for the delightful heat in her blood caused by this man's arms around her, this man's body sheltering her, waking the desire that had long lain dormant, making her want to lose herself in passion.

The music stopped. They stood still, two figures frozen in time. And then the music started again and they moved in rhythm, unspeaking, eyes closed, not dancing but holding, touching. His fingers played on her spine. Hers slid down to cup the taut slope of his buttocks beneath his tunic. His lips fluttered over her temple. She put her mouth to the rough skin of his throat. He was aroused. It had been so long since she had experienced the delicious frisson of such intimacy. So very, very long since she had even thought about it.

He was thinking about it, too. He could have stopped dancing at the last song, at the one before or the one before that, but each time the music started up again he pulled her closer. Then the music stopped for the last time, and they were left alone on the dance floor.

"I don't want to let you go," Robbie said, "not just yet."

"Then walk me back to my apartment," Sylvie said, without even considering the dangers of being alone with this stranger, a stranger who had been trained to kill without compunction. A man who represented all she hated and all that had damaged her life irrevocably. A soldier. A warmonger. But tonight, she found that she didn't want to be alone either.

Don't miss
NEVER FORGET ME,
available from Harlequin® Historical
August 2014.

HARLEQUIN®

HISTORICAL

Where love is timeless

COMING IN AUGUST 2014

Beguiled by Her Betrayer
by Louise Allen

WHAT USE ARE DRAWING-ROOM MANNERS IN THE MIDDLE OF THE DESERT?

Falling unconscious in the Egyptian sand at Cleo Valsac's feet is *not* part of Lord Quintus Bredon Deverall's plan. He's *supposed* to be whisking this young widow away from her father's dusty camp and back to England—to her aristocratic grandfather and a respectable husband.

Despite her strong-willed nature, Cleo can't help but feel comforted by Quin's protective presence. But she has no idea of this wounded stranger's true identity…or of the passion that will begin to burn between them under the heat of the desert sun!

Available wherever books and ebooks are sold.

HARLEQUIN®

HISTORICAL

Where love is timeless

COMING IN AUGUST 2014
Salvation in the Rancher's Arms
by Kelly Boyce

**HE HAD MORE THE EDGE OF AN OUTLAW —
THAN A SHINING KNIGHT.**

Rachel Sutter's world is turned upside down when Caleb Beckett rides into Salvation Falls. He brings news of a poker game gone disastrously wrong—not only has her wastrel husband been killed, he's also gambled away Rachel's home!

Suddenly, Rachel is left with nothing but an unpaid debt, and Caleb is holding all the cards—not to mention the deed to her land. There's something about the enigmatic drifter that she is instinctively drawn to, but how can she begin to trust him when so much of his past is shrouded in mystery?

Available wherever books and ebooks are sold.

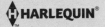
HARLEQUIN®

ℋISTORICAL

Where love is timeless

COMING IN AUGUST 2014

The Rake's Ruined Lady
by **Mary Brendan**

DISHONORABLE INTENTIONS ON HIS MIND!

Beatrice Dewey keeps falling for unsuitable men. She believes
the man she loved, Hugh Kendrick, is lost to her forever, and now
her new fiancé has canceled their wedding!

But then Hugh reenters her life, trailing rumors of illicit love
affairs in his wake. Instead of marriage, he offers her a very public,
passionate kiss! To succumb to his skillful seduction would be the
ultimate road to ruin, but is there enough of the old Hugh left to
convince Bea to give him another chance?

Available wherever books and ebooks are sold.

HH29796R